The Draconia Novels

Dragon Riders
The Egg That Wouldn't Hatch
Dragon Magic
The Dragon Who Chooses Twice
The Girl, the Gryphon, and the Dragon
The Mage's Dilemma
The Seer's Challenge
The Dragon and the Unicorn

The Dragonwind Novels

The Fox, the Stag, and the Dragon
Dragon Sanctuary

DRAGON SANCTUARY

DRAGON SANCTUARY

DAPHNE ASHLING PURPUS

Purpus Publishing, Vashon, WA

Some believe it is only great power that can hold evil in check, but that is not what I have found. It is the small everyday deeds of ordinary folk that keep the darkness at bay. Small acts of kindness and love. Why Bilbo Baggins? Perhaps because I am afraid, and he gives me courage.

—J. R. R. Tolkien

Contents

List of Characters · xi
Chapter 1 Escape · 1
Chapter 2 Hiding · 9
Chapter 3 Critical Injuries · · · · · · · · · · · · · · · · · · · 17
Chapter 4 Crisis · 23
Chapter 5 Healing · 33
Chapter 6 Nightmares · 39
Chapter 7 New Friends · 45
Chapter 8 Mine Collapse · 53
Chapter 9 Refugees · 61
Chapter 10 Threats · 69
Chapter 11 Treasure · 75
Chapter 12 The Capital · 81
Chapter 13 Nighttime Raids · · · · · · · · · · · · · · · · · 89
Chapter 14 Safety Measures · · · · · · · · · · · · · · · · · 93
Chapter 15 Scouting Reports · · · · · · · · · · · · · · · · ·101
Chapter 16 Historical Archives · · · · · · · · · · · · · · ·107
Chapter 17 Dragon Lessons · · · · · · · · · · · · · · · · ·113
Chapter 18 Village Changes · · · · · · · · · · · · · · · · ·119
Chapter 19 Challenges ·127
Chapter 20 Repercussions · · · · · · · · · · · · · · · · · ·141
Chapter 21 Confrontations · · · · · · · · · · · · · · · · ·151
Chapter 22 Battle ·157
Chapter 23 Resolution ·165
About the Author ·175

LIST OF CHARACTERS

Aloysius: Estrea's most learned historian. He lives in the palace, in the turret where the archives are stored.

Angelica: An infant from the mining towns. Her grandfather is Rob.

Berimund: A large brown bear.

Bruce: The twelve-year-old son of Lord Gofrond's foreman.

Criseda: A teenage female turquoise dragon.

Dragonwind: Ty's village, which is near the dragons' aerie.

Drake: A villager from Dragonwind who is against helping refugees.

Elfrida: A retired schoolteacher living in Dragonwind.

Ernest: Youngest son of King Bertram and Queen Elicia, six months old.

Esme: A thirteen-year-old girl with magical gifts who has been abused and tortured by her parents since she was five years old.

Esther: Esme's abusive mother.

Estrea: The nation ruled by King Bertram, which contains the village of Dragonwind.

Foster: A male green dragon.

Foxy: A black cat who lives with Ty.

George: A Dragonwind villager.

Harriet: Three-year-old twin daughter of King Bertram and Queen Elicia.

Hazel: Three-year-old twin daughter of King Bertram and Queen Elicia.

Henry: The steward at King Bertram's palace.

Jeb: The gamekeeper for the forests around Dragonwind. He and Ty are best friends.

Johnston: The mine superintendent for Lord Upworth.

King Bertram: King of Estrea. He is married to Queen Elicia. They have three sons and two daughters.

King Joseph: King of Mlinred.

Kyle: An old hermit living in Dragonwind.

Lance: Nine-year-old son of King Bertram and Queen Elicia.

Lord Gofrond: A member of King Bertram's council of advisers.

Lord Osterfels: The illegitimate half brother of King Bertram who had Ty's parents killed.

Lord Plumfield: A noble from the neighboring nation of Mlinred.

Lord Upworth: A member of King Bertram's council of advisers.

Magnolia: A large yellow female dragon.

Malcolm: King Bertram's fifteen-year-old nephew, son of Lady Priscilla.

Martha: Bakery owner and healer who is granted guardianship of Esme by King Bertram.

Mirabella: A brown rabbit.

Miranda: A female red fox who is a friend to Ty.

Mlinred: A neighboring nation, where Lord Plumfield lives.

Naomi: A young woman from one of the mining villages who is the mother of Paul.

Paul: A boy from the mining villages who was injured in a mine collapse and who has telepathic abilities.

Oscar: A young orange male dragon with yellow wings.

Queen Elicia: Married to King Bertram. They have three sons and two daughters.

Ralph: Six-year-old son of Wilson and Selena.

Raymond: Fifteen-year-old son of King Bertram and Queen Elicia, the eldest and Bertram's heir.

Roy: A seven-year-old redheaded boy working in the mines.

Rob: An old man who used to work in the mines. He's Angelica's grandfather.

Rupert: A male red fox living in the fields outside the palace. He runs the fox telepathic network between King Bertram in the palace and Ty in Dragonwind. He is friends with Samantha and Esme.

Rutherglen: A small hamlet just outside the capital. Esme and her family live here.

Samantha: A gray squirrel who is a friend of both Rupert and Esme.

Sapphire: A bluish-purple female dragon and the dragons' leader.

Sara: A resident of Dragonwind and Martha's best friend.

Selena: A former resident of one of the mining villages, married to the carpenter, Wilson, and mother of a six-year-old son, Ralph.

Silas: The castle arms master.

Stephen: Esme's abusive father.

The Wraith: A powerful unknown villain, with his own secret network of henchmen. He's thought to be a person of power, wealth, and influence.

Thomas: A twelve-year-old orphan boy.

Tim: An old man who used to work in the mines.

Tobias: An ancient philosopher who has studied the legends and stories of Estrea.

Ty: The leader of Dragonwind. He is telepathic, has a special bond with the dragons, and can do healing magic.

White Star: Ty's horse, a roan mare with a white star on her forehead.

Wilhelmina: A moose living in the forests northeast of Dragonwind.

Wilson: A carpenter from one of the small mining villages who leaves the village with his wife, Selena, and their six-year-old son, Ralph.

CHAPTER 1

ESCAPE

Esme stood by the barred window in her tiny bedroom on a windy autumn night, nervously chewing on a fingernail. Once again, she had an escape plan. She couldn't remember just how many of them she'd tried in her thirteen years, but this really was her last chance. This plan couldn't fail.

She listened carefully to the night sounds. Hours ago, her parents had shoved a meager dinner through a flap in her door, a door that had been reinforced after one of her escape attempts and that was always kept locked and bolted. She had heard them go upstairs to their room at least three hours ago, and now she could hear her father's snoring.

Otherwise, there were no sounds from within the house. Esme remembered all too well the time when she was five and had innocently told her mother that it wasn't nice to hurt people. She hadn't realized then that not everyone could hear the thoughts of others, that her mother hadn't spoken aloud. Esme had a magical gift, although all these years later, she didn't really think of it as a gift but rather as a curse.

Her parents worked for a very evil man, known only as The Wraith, and when he realized her talent, he made sure her parents used her to learn the secrets of all the villagers in the hamlet of Rutherglen. Over the years, Esme's resistance to her parents had grown, and she'd managed to protect many, giving up only minor information, but that was getting harder to do. The Wraith was not satisfied, and he'd threatened her parents, who in turn had taken to beating and nearly starving her.

A week ago, Esme had learned by reading her parents' thoughts that The Wraith was going to arrive in three days and that he was going to take her away and deal with her directly. So now there was no choice but to make a successful escape.

Esme had a major advantage that thankfully no one else knew about. She could communicate telepathically with animals. In fact, her friend Rupert, a red fox, had helped her make her current escape plan, and Samantha, a gray squirrel, was assisting as well.

It's time, said Rupert. *Samantha has looked into your parents' bedroom window, and they're sound asleep. Ready?*

Yes, said Esme. *Let's do it.*

With that, Esme took her flint and carefully worked to light a small pile of tinder on her windowsill. Rupert and Samantha had been gathering fuel for the past few days. They stuffed a bit through the bars on her window, and the rest was piled up outside against the wall, under the window. The plan required setting the wall on fire so that the bars would fall out as the window burned. It was a dangerous plan, one that could very well get her killed, and she knew that. But she also knew that she could never allow herself to be taken to The Wraith. It would be better to be dead.

Carefully, Esme nursed the little spark of flame until it was big enough to catch a few longer pieces on fire. Then she dropped the burning sticks through the window as Rupert and Samantha guided them onto the materials they had gathered. The wind had picked up, which helped to fan the flames.

Soon the wall was on fire. Esme grabbed a small pack and tried to push on the bars of the window, but she quickly realized that she wasn't going to budge the bars without seriously burning her hands. Rupert and Samantha were working on the outside of the wall. Rupert was able to use a sturdy branch to pry at the bars, and once he had the branch in place, both he and Samantha pushed on it.

Esme started to kick at the wall. She could feel the heat radiating from the fire, and smoke was blowing into her room. She got down on the floor, on her back, as close to the wall as she dared, and then kicked hard with both feet at the same time.

Suddenly she heard a crack, and Rupert called, *The wall is burning through.*

Esme scrambled to her feet and looked in horror as the entire wall seemed to crumble. Rupert yelled, *Jump now!*

Esme didn't stop to think. She grabbed her pack, ran at the opening, and jumped through the flames into the yard outside her window. Rupert and Samantha pounded on her to put out the flames that had singed her clothes, and soon the three of them were running for the forest. They heard a loud crash and turned around to see that the house was engulfed in flames and that the second floor had crashed down through what had been Esme's room.

That was too close, said Rupert.

I agree, said Esme.

They turned again to the forest as Esme's father, Stephen, tore out of the house, followed closely by her mother, Esther. The two of them were shouting angrily at her. Esme didn't pause; she kept running as fast as she could.

But her father was faster, and he was gaining on them. Rupert said, *You two keep going. I'll stop him.*

How? asked Esme.

Don't worry; just run!

With that, Esme and Samantha ran as hard as they could as Rupert turned to face Stephen.

Stephen didn't seem at all concerned by the fox, but as he tried to run past Rupert, Rupert snarled and leaped. He caught Stephen's left arm and bit down hard. Stephen howled in pain and shook his arm vigorously, but Rupert refused to let go.

Stephen ran to a tree and then swung his arm so that he'd smash Rupert against the large trunk, but Rupert was too smart for him. Just as Stephen swung, Rupert let go, dropped to the ground, and then grabbed onto Stephen's right leg, again biting down with the full strength of his jaws.

Stephen tried to kick Rupert with his left leg but managed only to fall down. Rupert let go of the leg and instead jumped onto Rupert's face, scratching at his eyes and biting his nose clean through.

Esther was running toward them now, so Rupert took off to follow Esme and Samantha. *Esme,* he called, *I'm coming now. Your dad won't be following for a while.*

Rupert caught up with Esme and Samantha, and the three of them continued through the woods. Esme was too tired to run. She had some burns, and she'd reached the end of her strength. Rupert said, *I think we should make for the palace.*

The palace? said Esme. *Where King Bertram lives? Why?*

King Bertram knows me, and he'll help. I know he will.

I don't know, said Esme. *I'm just a kid, and The Wraith has real power. No one seems to know who he is, but my parents always said that he was a really important person, even though they didn't know his true identity.*

That may be, said Rupert, *but the king knows me. I've helped him before, and the king can speak with me. We may not know who The Wraith is, but I'm betting that King Bertram will be able to send you somewhere safe.*

I trust you and Samantha, said Esme, *but I don't know about anyone else.*

OK, said Rupert, *how would it be if I found a place for you and Samantha to hide near the palace, and I went and talked to King Bertram by myself, not giving your name or location, but just telling him about your situation? Then I could see what he thinks and come back to report to you.*

Esme hesitated. She wasn't sure what to do. She'd never managed to get this far away from her parents in all her escape attempts. Finally, she said, *Can you hide us somewhere where I can see King Bertram as you two talk? I can then read his mind to discover if he's telling the truth.*

Yes, I can do that. He and I always meet in his back garden, and there's a shed there that you and Samantha can hide behind.

Esme nodded, and the three of them set off again. Esme couldn't run anymore or even walk very fast, so their pace was considerably slower. Dawn was breaking when Rupert finally led them into the back palace garden. He showed Esme and Samantha where to stand and then walked over to a nearby bench and called to King Bertram. *King Bertram, Rupert here. I need your help.*

I'll be right there, Bertram answered.

Esme watched as the king came out of the back door of the palace and walked over to the bench. She saw that he was tall and slim, and she felt that

4

he had a kind heart. She sensed no deception or falseness in him, but she waited, hidden, as Rupert talked with him.

I need your help, began Rupert. *Do you remember I told you about a friend of mine who has been abused by her parents?*

Yes, answered Bertram, and Esme started. She hadn't realized that Rupert had confided in anyone.

Well, we had to help her escape tonight, Samantha and I. She was incredibly brave, fleeing through a burning wall as her home collapsed from the fire she set. Her parents chased after us, but I stopped them, and now we've reached you.

Rupert paused and looked toward the shed where Esme and Samantha were hiding. Slowly, Esme stepped out from behind the shed and moved closer to Rupert.

King Bertram stayed sitting on the bench but smiled as he looked at her. Then he said, "How can I help you?"

Esme was silent for a minute, then she blurted out, "My parents were planning to hand me over to The Wraith. Do you know about him?"

King Bertram said, "I'm starting to hear rumors, but why don't you tell me what you know?"

"I only know what my parents know. I realize it's an invasion of privacy to listen into anyone's thoughts without them knowing, but somehow, I don't feel guilty about doing it with them because, after all, that's what they wanted me to do to others."

"I think that's very appropriate," said King Bertram, his voice radiating kindness and sympathy.

"What I learned is that The Wraith keeps his identity concealed. He wears a mask and black cloak, disguises his voice, and most of the time sends his underlings to deliver messages. He is reputed to be someone really powerful in your government, and he lives in the capital."

"That's disturbing," said King Bertram, "but you aren't the first to suggest that."

"He's ruthless, and my parents are really scared of him. He's had them blackmailing people with whatever information they can force me to divulge. I've tried really hard, ever since I was old enough to understand what they were doing, to give only the most harmless information, but sometimes it's difficult to resist my father's torture."

"That's a burden you should never have had to carry," said King Bertram. "I will keep you safe, I promise."

"How?" asked Esme. "We don't even know who The Wraith is or who his underlings are."

"Obviously we need to get you out of the capital," said King Bertram. "I would like to have Rupert and Samantha escort you to Dragonwind, near the dragon sanctuary, where my ambassador, Ty, and his dragon, Criseda, live. There are others in Dragonwind whom I trust as well, most notably Martha, who raised Ty after his parents were killed and who owns the bakery, and Kyle, a hermit who has helped us before and who now is courting Martha. You'll be safe there for sure."

Esme thought for a bit. "I think you should know that The Wraith is hurting a lot of others, many of them my age or even younger. My parents know of other parents whose children have gone missing, and the rumor is that The Wraith is kidnapping them as child labor to work down in his mines. He needs small bodies to get through his tunnels."

"That needs to be stopped," said King Bertram. "Do you know anything else about his activities?"

"My father was sure that The Wraith killed anyone who either disobeyed him or tried to find out who he was. If people didn't hand over their tribute to The Wraith, they were given two days to come up with what they owed if it was the first time they missed. If they didn't pay in two days, they were killed. If it was the second time, they were killed right away."

"He really does rule by fear, doesn't he?" said Bertram.

"My parents aren't scared of anyone, but they are terrified of The Wraith."

"We need to get you to safety at once," said King Bertram. "I don't want anyone knowing that we've even talked. Rupert, can you get her to Ty safely?"

Yes, answered Rupert, who like other telepathic creatures was able to understand human speech and had followed Esme's discussion with King Bertram, so that both Esme and Bertram could hear him. *We'll activate the fox telepathic link again as we have before. We can keep in touch with you that way, and once I get the message through to Miranda, she'll take care of everything in Dragonwind.*

6

"How long will it take you to get there?" asked the king.

To do it safely, we're going to take a circuitous route, so it will probably take us two weeks. I don't want a direct line to Dragonwind for Esme's safety. It may take her parents, especially her father, a day or two to recover from my attack, but I also expect that her father will be very angry—he's missing a large chunk of his nose now, in addition to some nasty bites—and I also expect that The Wraith will force them to find her.

"I know you're right," said Bertram. "Esme, you have a very special and unusual gift, being able not only to read minds but also to determine the character of those you come in contact with, and that's a talent The Wraith would find irresistible. He can't afford to let you go. You aren't just slave labor."

Esme bit her fingernails and trembled a bit. "I don't know why I can do what I do, but I wish I couldn't."

"Ty will help you with your gift, as will Kyle and Criseda, but for now I can see why you're scared. Being different is never easy, and you've been abused by those who should have protected you. I'm going to see that your parents are punished, but I can't do that right away because they can't know that you've found protection."

Esme didn't look very convinced, but she was silent. Then Rupert said, *Can you get a message to Ty? I'd feel better if I knew that he and Criseda would keep an eye out for us. I know they fly over Estrea all the time so no one need know why they're in the sky, but we do have a long way to go, and I sure don't trust either Esme's parents or The Wraith, who's probably got expert trackers at his beck and call.*

"That's a good idea," said Bertram. "I would have them come pick you up, Esme, but I don't want to take a chance that anyone knows where you've gone. So you'll have a long walk, but I do think that's safer."

Esme nodded as Rupert said, *We'll be off now. Good luck trying to figure out who The Wraith is. None of us will rest easy until he's caught.*

With that, the three turned to go as King Bertram called softly, "Good luck to you all."

CHAPTER 2

HIDING

Esme followed Rupert and Samantha as they headed out of the palace gardens and into the woods again. She was very tired and hungry. Rupert didn't go far before he said, *I know where there's a cave nearby where we can rest until late afternoon. And we need to eat. Just hang on for a little longer, and we'll take a break.*

I'll try, answered Esme as she staggered onward. She was so tired, and she realized that she had burns from the fire that were hurting now that she wasn't running for her life. She was glad she could talk telepathically because she didn't even have the energy to speak.

Rupert was true to his word. Before long, he was leading them into a large cave. Rupert called out, *Berimund, are you here?*

Esme was startled to see a large brown bear coming toward them from the rear of the cave. *Hi, Rupert, Samantha,* said the bear. *Who's your friend?*

Esme just stared as Rupert introduced her and then explained that they had to travel secretly to Ty in Dragonwind.

Doesn't look as if you're going to go anywhere until that little one gets some rest and food, said Berimund.

Esme wanted to say that she wasn't a little one. After all, she was thirteen, but she was too tired and, of course, compared to the enormous bear, she was little. Her parents had never given her much food, and lately they'd thought she'd be more cooperative if they starved her, so she was really lacking in strength.

9

Berimund turned to the back of his cave, motioning for Esme to follow. He led her to a large nesting area, and Esme sank down on the moss and fern fronds gratefully. She fell asleep almost instantly.

It was late afternoon when Esme woke. Berimund was standing beside her with an earthen bowl filled with honey and a large slab of bread. *Here you go, little one,* Berimund said. She sat up, and he handed her the food.

She ate ravenously and then, remembering her manners, said, *Thank you. How did you get such delicious bread?*

Berimund chuckled. *I have human friends, and they love to bake things for me in exchange for the honey I get for them.*

Once Esme had eaten, Berimund said, *Rupert and Samantha are out in the woods looking for a good route, and they're also checking to see if there's anyone pursuing you. They'll be back soon with their report.*

Esme nodded and sat quietly next to Berimund. She felt safe next to the bear, but she was also really worried. She knew her parents, and they would never give up looking for her, not because they cared about her, but because The Wraith would demand it. They feared The Wraith more than anything else in the world.

It wasn't long before Rupert and Samantha returned. Rupert said, *We haven't seen anyone, but we'd better get out of here now anyway. Are you ready?*

Esme nodded and stood up. Then she gave Berimund a big hug and said, *Thank you.*

Berimund hugged her back, and as Esme, Rupert, and Samantha left his cave, he said, *I'll wipe out your tracks, and I'll also lay a false trail going in another direction. I don't know how long that will fool them, but it might help and give you a chance to get away.*

Thanks, said Rupert.

Esme, Rupert, and Samantha hiked for hours through the woods. It was dark, and without Rupert and Samantha to help her, Esme would have gone in circles. But she trusted them to guide her. Their progress was not very fast because Esme had trouble navigating in the dark and tripped frequently. She also wasn't very strong, having spent most of her life locked in her tiny bedroom.

Finally, as dawn was beginning to break, Rupert found them shelter, and Esme collapsed in exhaustion leaning against a fir tree. She was asleep almost instantly.

Rupert and Samantha looked down at her, and Samantha said, *It's going to take a lot longer to get to Dragonwind with her, isn't it? She's just not strong enough, although she sure is determined.*

I'm afraid so, said Rupert. *And the longer we're on the run, the greater the chance that we'll be caught.*

What are we going to do? asked Samantha.

I'm not sure, said Rupert. *For now, we need to keep moving. We also need to scavenge for food. But one of us needs to stay with Esme at all times. Do you want to scavenge first or guard Esme?*

I'll hunt for food. You can plan. I'm wondering if we'd be better off now moving during the day. It wouldn't be as hard on Esme, said Samantha.

I guess you're right, said Rupert. *Let's give her the morning to sleep, and then we'll leave right after we eat if you can find us something.*

Be back soon, said Samantha as she raced off.

Rupert patrolled the area around the secluded glen that he'd found. It wasn't as secure as a cave, but he couldn't hear any signs of pursuit. He'd hoped to take a roundabout route to Dragonwind, but now he was afraid that that would take far too long. He needed to get close enough to Dragonwind to be able to contact Ty. He trusted Ty to know what the best plan was. It hadn't seemed so hard when he was talking with King Bertram, but no one had realized just how weak Esme was.

Samantha returned just before noon, and she'd managed to find both nuts and berries. She'd eaten her share before returning so that she'd be able to carry more for Rupert and Esme. Rupert gently woke Esme, and while they ate, Rupert said, *I think I should tell you a bit about Ty and Dragonwind so that you know more about where we're going.*

Rupert continued. *Ty was only a small child when both of his parents were killed on the orders of Lord Osterfels, a nasty man who had a big estate in Dragonwind and made life miserable for everyone. Ty was known then as Thyra. He'd been born into a girl's body but he always knew he was a boy. He hid from Lord Osterfels by changing his name to Ty and pretending to be a distant male relation of Martha, who then raised him. The only ones who knew were Martha, who'd been a good friend of Ty's parents, and Jeb, Ty's best friend.*

It took a long time, until Ty was seventeen, for him to get the proof to convict Lord Osterfels, the illegitimate half brother of King Bertram, of his parents' murders, but he did it, with help from friends. Ty is also telepathic, and that's helped him. And he's made friends with the dragons. In fact, once Lord Osterfels and one of his twin sons were convicted of a lot of crimes, including the imprisonment and attempted murder of Lord Osterfels's wife and his other son, the dragons granted Ty a tremendous boon: they changed his body to match his real self. In addition, King Bertram granted him all of Lord Osterfels's holdings and now Ty keeps watch over Dragonwind and all its peoples.

So you see, Esme, Ty will look after you, and he knows better than most what it is to have magical talents and to be different from others. You'll be safe with him and Martha.

Esme nodded, and with that, they trudged onward.

We've decided not to walk at night, Rupert told Esme, *so if you can just keep going for a few hours, until it's dark, then you can have a full night's sleep, I promise.*

OK, said Esme. *Sorry I can't go faster.*

Not your fault, said Samantha. *Actually, I think you're amazing! You escaped and you've kept going, even though we know it's really hard for you. We're going to do this.*

The afternoon wore on as Esme concentrated on putting one foot in front of the other. She couldn't remember ever being so tired. But she knew that they were all in tremendous danger, and whatever else happened, she wasn't going back.

Samantha caught sight of a family of squirrels, and she called to them, chattering away in squirrel talk. She explained their need for a safe place to stay for the night and for their need for food, especially for Esme.

The family of squirrels ran off once Samantha had talked to them, and Samantha told Esme and Rupert, *They know of a cave not too far away. They also have been befriended by a farmer's wife, and they'll try to get us some food. We just need to keep walking in this direction, and they'll find us once they've arranged things.*

That's great, said Rupert.

Esme just nodded; she was too tired to talk.

After about an hour, the squirrels were back, and they showed them the way to a small cave in the side of a hill. The squirrels had put some bread and cheese and a flask of water inside the cave.

Samantha thanked them before asking, *Have you seen any trackers in this area? There could be some really bad people hunting for us.*

No, we haven't, said the father of the squirrel family, *but if you want, we can keep a lookout tonight so you all can sleep.*

Rupert said, *We'd really appreciate that.*

The next morning Rupert, Esme, and Samantha said goodbye to the squirrel family after breakfast and headed out of the glen. Rupert had decided that today they needed to aim for the mountains to the northeast. He knew this would be a harder path, but there was no easy way to get to Dragonwind.

Esme did not complain about the difficulties but just continued to try her best. She was quite short for her age and rail thin, but she climbed up the path with all the strength she could muster.

The three of them had taken a break around midday to eat some more nuts and berries that Samantha had managed to find when they were startled by a vulture flying overhead and landing in a nearby tree.

That can't be a good sign, said Rupert.

The vulture flew off after a few minutes, heading back toward the capital, but Rupert was worried. He sent out many telepathic calls for help, especially to Ty, but he wasn't sure if any of them were heard. He did manage to contact a fox in the fox communication network who promised to send his plea for help on to Miranda in Dragonwind.

Rupert pushed Esme as fast as he dared. They were out in the open on a mountainside on a path that had a steep drop-off on the right side, and he wasn't sure when or where they'd find a secure shelter. The three of them moved as quickly as poor Esme could manage. By late afternoon, they were exhausted, but they had covered more ground.

Then Esme stopped with a look of terror on her face. *Someone's following us,* she said.

Rupert and Samantha listened carefully, and at first they couldn't hear anything, but then the sound of other hikers was unmistakable. Rupert couldn't find a good hiding spot, and before they knew it, Stephen was leading a group of four men toward them.

Stephen yelled at them to stop as he raised a bow to fire on them. He aimed straight for Rupert and said, "I'll get you, you piece of vermin."

Rupert stood his ground, but Esme stepped in front of Rupert just as the arrow fired. The arrow hit her in her right leg, and she crumpled to the ground. Rupert and Samantha headed into the bushes, realizing that they could do nothing against five men.

Stephen ran to Esme and yanked the arrow out of her leg. He then tied a dirty rag around it to stop the bleeding and told her to stand. She was crying now and didn't move, so he yanked her to her feet.

"You've caused me more trouble than you're worth," he yelled. "You burned our home to the ground. That stupid fox cost me most of my nose, not to mention other bites. Your mother just laughs at me. I'm not going to stand for your rebellion anymore."

Then he shoved her, telling her to get moving. However, when he pushed her, he caused her to lose her balance. She stumbled, and as Rupert watched in horror, she fell off the edge of the path, reeling down the cliff face.

Stephen yelled at her. "You aren't getting away that easily." Then he told two of the men to get down the side of the cliff and drag her back up again.

The men grumbled, but they knew better than to disobey Stephen. Everyone knew that Stephen was under orders from The Wraith. They slid and stumbled down the side of the cliff, trying to find Esme. She'd fallen badly and banged her head on a large rock. One of the men grabbed Esme and threw her over his shoulder, and then the men struggled back up to the path.

Rupert and Samantha watched but couldn't figure out any way to help Esme. Rupert kept calling telepathically for help from any creatures who were nearby. At first, he didn't get any replies, but then he started to see squirrels, rabbits, and a flock of crows heading toward them. The men didn't even notice, at least not at first, but Rupert and Samantha headed out of the bushes to add to the numbers. The squirrels leaped onto the men, scratching and biting. The rabbits managed to trip the men as they tried to get rid of the squirrels. Possibly the most effective, though, were the crows, who flew straight at the men's faces and pecked at their eyes.

Soon the men were screaming. The man who was holding Esme dropped her in his efforts to dislodge a crow from his face. The men were stumbling around so much that they lost sight of the edge of the path. Two of them fell over the edge. Rupert tried to get close to Esme. He wasn't sure he could move her or indeed if she should even be moved, but he wanted to guard her.

Then everyone looked up as a loud trumpeting sound came from above. Rupert saw Ty, riding on Criseda, a gorgeous turquoise dragon. The sight of Ty on Criseda was the final straw for the men. The two who had fallen over the edge were scrambling to go farther down, and Stephen and the other two who were still on the path took off running. As soon as they did so, the squirrels, rabbits, and crows left off their attack and instead circled around Esme to protect her.

Criseda was too big to land on the path, but she hovered just above it so that Ty could climb down. Ty jumped from Criseda's front leg and went immediately to Esme.

Rupert told Ty, *She took an arrow meant for me, and then her own father tried to force her to stand, but she couldn't move fast enough for him. He shoved her, and she went over the edge of the path. She's hurt very badly.*

Ty, a tall, slim young man with short brown hair and deep brown eyes, bent over Esme and quickly examined her. *Rupert, you and Samantha need to get back to King Bertram and let him know what's happened. Criseda and I will carry Esme on to Dragonwind and get her medical help. It looks as if she's got some broken bones in addition to the arrow wound and probably a concussion.*

Can't we go with you? We want to be with Esme, said Rupert.

I understand, Ty said, *and if King Bertram says it's OK, you can come to Dragonwind to be with her after you report to him. But he has to know what just happened. I know Bertram hoped that you would be able to get to Dragonwind in secret, but now that those villains have seen Criseda and me, they're going to know just where she is. That's going to make it harder to keep her safe, and King Bertram needs that information.*

Rupert went over to Esme and licked her cheek, then he turned to Ty and nodded. *We'll do it, and we'll be fast. With any luck, you'll see us in Dragonwind before very long.*

With that, he and Samantha turned to look at all the creatures who'd come to their aid and said, *Thank you all so much!* Then they took off running down the path.

Ty looked at the group of squirrels, rabbits, and crows and smiled. *You guys are absolutely the best. Criseda and I couldn't get here as fast as you did, and you kept those men from harming Esme even more. Whenever you're in Dragonwind, be sure to say hi.*

Ty gently picked up Esme and lifted her high above his head so that Criseda could grab her with her front legs. Then Ty vaulted up onto Criseda's back, and they took off for Dragonwind.

CHAPTER 3

CRITICAL INJURIES

As they flew to Dragonwind, Ty reached out telepathically to Esme. He was gifted with healing skills, and even with the little he'd seen of Esme's injuries, he knew he'd be hard pressed to save her. The most he could do now as they flew was try to stabilize her.

Criseda interrupted his efforts. *Where should I take us?*

That's a good question, answered Ty. *My first thought is to take her to Martha's, as she has more healing skills than anyone else, except me, and I'm going to need someone to add to my abilities or we'll lose Esme. Kyle can also help, as he has a lot of wisdom. But if we take her into Dragonwind, we won't be able to keep her presence a secret.*

Do you think there are enemies in Dragonwind? asked Criseda.

We're just beginning to uncover the extent of The Wraith's organization, said Ty. *I know Dragonwind is a long way from the capital, but even so, The Wraith could have henchmen in Dragonwind.*

Where else could we take her? asked Criseda.

My home, said Ty, *or the dragons'. No one would dare breach the dragons' stronghold.*

True, said Criseda, *but you know the rules as well as I do. Dragons won't assist humans unless the fate of the planet is at stake. They won't allow you to hide Esme there if it's seen as a power struggle between two humans or two groups, even though The Wraith is so obviously undesirable and even though they like what King Bertram is doing for his nation.*

They've allowed you to stay with me, said Ty.

Yes, but I'm to be a liaison between our worlds, said Criseda. *I'm only an impartial observer. If I overstep my instructions, I will no longer be allowed to work with you.*

So where do we take Esme? asked Ty.

I think your original notion to take her to Martha is still the best, said Criseda. *We'll just have to be very vigilant and keep them all safe.*

OK, said Ty. *I don't like it. It seems as if we're painting a target on Esme and Martha, but I can't think of anywhere else she can get the medical help she so desperately needs.*

They flew in silence after that and soon landed behind Martha's cottage and bakery. Ty lifted Esme carefully and quietly and took her into Martha's kitchen, using the back door as he always did. As soon as he was inside, Criseda took off and flew back to Ty's home, a cave in the mountains about halfway between Dragonwind and the dragons' lair.

Martha and Kyle were sitting in the kitchen having tea when Ty walked in. Martha jumped up and said, "Ty, what's happened?"

"I have a really sick and injured young lady who needs all of our help."

"You know the way," said Martha as she hurried to her herb cabinet. "Take her to my guest room."

Kyle stood and went ahead of Ty so that he could turn down the bed. Ty carefully laid Esme on the sheets. She looked so small.

"What happened?" asked Kyle as Martha came in with a bowl of warm water, towels, and various herbs.

"It's a very sad story. Briefly, Esme has telepathic gifts that her parents and others have abused for years. She finally escaped, but then her father and a bunch of thugs caught up with her. Rupert and Samantha did their best, along with a host of other woodland creatures, and then Criseda scared the men off."

As Ty was relating this, Martha worked over Esme, trying to determine the extent of her injuries.

"Has she regained consciousness since she hit her head?" Martha asked.

"Not that we know of," answered Ty.

"That's a nasty bump on her head. The arrow wound in her leg is bad too. Looks as if it was a barbed arrow. The other leg is broken, and I suspect that a couple ribs are also at least cracked. You two, help me get her undressed. It's probably a good thing that she's unconscious, at least for the moment."

Ty and Kyle lifted Esme and pulled off her clothes down to her underpants. As they turned her to get the clothes off, Martha gasped in horror. "Look at her back," she exclaimed. "These scars are a mix of old and current. What has this poor child been through?"

"She's so thin," said Kyle. "Her ribs are sticking out. How old did you say she is?"

"Rupert told King Bertram that she's thirteen," said Ty, "but she sure doesn't look it. She has not started developing at all, and she's very short for her age."

"I'd love to get my hands on whoever did this," said Martha as she began to bathe Esme.

Ty said, "From what I've learned, she was kept locked up in a tiny bedroom, starved, and then beaten if she didn't give her parents the information they wanted. There was a blackmail ring involved."

"Blackmail is so destructive. Remember what it did to Dragonwind," said Martha.

"I do," said Ty.

"I'm going to need splints," said Martha.

"I'll get them," offered Kyle.

"Thanks," said Ty. "I'm going to try to add my healing magic to your work, Martha."

"That's good because I'm not sure my skills are enough to save her. The damage is so extensive. Please check for any internal bleeding if you can."

Kyle left the room to find splints. Ty knelt beside Esme on the side of the bed away from Martha so that he wouldn't be in her way, closed his eyes, and began sending his healing thoughts toward Esme, searching for injuries.

He was horrified to discover how many wounds Esme had, some going back to when she was a tiny little girl. He couldn't heal them all, at least not quickly, so he did as Martha had suggested and searched for life-threatening injuries.

He discovered two cracked ribs, as Martha had suspected, and he mended them, at least to the point where they wouldn't get worse. He found some internal bleeding and swelling in her head, and he carefully cauterized the wounds to stop the bleeding. The swelling would take time to recede, but it shouldn't get worse.

He looked at the arrow wound and saw that it was already showing signs of infection. He hoped that Martha's herbs would help there, as he was becoming very tired from expending so much healing magic. He had wished many times that his healing magic were stronger, but he had been able to heal things that Martha couldn't.

Kyle came in with two splints that he'd cut, and he and Martha got to work setting Esme's left leg. Ty went out to Martha's kitchen and made himself two sandwiches, which he ate quickly. He knew he needed food to refuel his magic, and he wanted to do more for Esme.

He went back into the guest room and sat by Esme to monitor her. Martha and Kyle had set the left leg, and Martha was wrapping Esme's chest to support the cracked ribs.

Ty looked at the arrow wound and was not happy to see how jagged it was. Martha had given it a preliminary cleaning, and it had stopped bleeding, but Ty could see that the ragged edges would need stitching. He used his magic to search for dirt deep in the wound. Finally, he asked Martha, "Do we dare try to soak this wound? I'm concerned about some dirt that I can feel deep inside it."

"I don't want to start up the bleeding," said Martha. "But I agree that we need to do something or infection will set in. I don't think Esme is strong enough to fight off an infection. The barbed arrow wasn't clean, and then her father used a filthy rag to bind it. I think that and the head wound are the most troublesome."

"I agree," said Ty. "The leg should be stitched, but that might just make things worse if we can't get it clean first."

"Exactly," said Martha. "Let me make some warm compresses, and we'll try that first."

Martha took her bowl and some bandages out to the kitchen to prepare the compresses. While she was out of the room, Kyle asked, "How much danger is Esme still in, aside from the injuries?"

"We'd hoped to get her here without The Wraith knowing where she went, but we were unsuccessful in that. Truth be told, it was an unrealistic hope, given how weak Esme was even before the encounter with her father on the trail. Rupert and Samantha said that Esme never complained and tried to move as quickly as she possibly could, but as you can see, her muscles are immature. She's been confined to a small room and never had the chance to develop properly. The escape and flight from her home, during which she showed incredible mental courage and a strong spirit, were just too much for her body."

"So her location is now known," said Kyle.

"Unfortunately, yes," said Ty. "We're going to have to keep watch over her. I know I can count on you, and I'm sure Jeb will want to help."

"Jeb was a victim of blackmail, so I'd imagine he'd be especially eager to stop another blackmailer."

"For sure," said Ty. "But otherwise, I think we should keep the number of people who know Esme's story to a minimum. I don't like to think of The Wraith having minions in Dragonwind, but his power seems to stretch far and wide. We have to be careful just who we trust."

"I don't want Martha in danger," said Kyle. "I think I'll insist that she let me stay here so that I can look after them both."

"Your days of being a reclusive hermit seem to be coming to a close," said Ty with a smile. "I'm really glad that you and Martha have reconnected after so many years."

"So am I," said Kyle. "I'm not used to being around folks, but I do enjoy working in Martha's bakery. Life takes some funny turns sometimes."

"That's for sure," said Ty. "I have to admit that I'm not sure where I'm going now after getting justice for my parents, but I'm grateful for Criseda and for King Bertram's faith in me. And now, it would seem, I'm meant to help another abuse victim, another human with magical talent. There aren't many of us, and somehow, those with special gifts seem to have a rougher time trying to find a path. I just hate how Esme has been used—and by her parents, who should have protected her."

"It's very sad," said Kyle. "And you're finding your way just fine. After all, you're only seventeen, and that's the right age for explorations. I'm sure you'll figure it out while you help Esme and others like her."

Martha bustled in with warm compresses and began applying them to Esme's right leg. "Ty, keep an eye on this with your magic and be sure we don't start up the bleeding again. A bit of bleeding to flush the wound is OK, but not a lot."

"Got it," said Ty as he began to monitor the leg with compresses.

As Martha predicted, the wound did begin bleeding some, but Ty hunted for the foreign dirt particles and nudged them into the slight flow without allowing the bleeding to increase. He and Martha had worked together before, and they made a good team.

Martha changed out the compresses several times until both she and Ty were certain that they'd gotten the wound as clean as they could. Then she sprinkled a special herb concoction into the wound and stitched it up. She applied clean bandages and finally stood up. "That's all we can do. Now we'll just have to watch her carefully for infections."

"Do you think we can try getting some liquids into her?" asked Kyle.

"I'm going to try dripping water from a sponge into her mouth first to see if she'll swallow. If she does, then we can slowly drip a nourishing broth into her," said Martha.

Ty stood as well. "I'm going to go find Jeb. Kyle and I talked about keeping a watch on Esme, but I think it should just be you, me, Kyle, and Jeb. It will make long hours for us, but I don't really trust anyone else."

"I understand," said Martha.

CHAPTER 4

CRISIS

Ty left Martha's cottage to go up into the mountains to his own home, a cave that he'd renovated with running water, a few pieces of furniture, and some wall hangings. He lived there with his black cat, Foxy, and it suited them well.

He went into the cave and called out to Foxy, *Hey, do you want to help me nurse a young girl back to health?*

Foxy was sleeping on Ty's bed in the back corner of the cave, but she stretched, jumped off the bed, and came over to rub up against Ty's legs. *Where is she? At Martha's?*

Yes, said Ty.

Then of course, answered Foxy. *Martha has great food!*

Ty bent down and scooped Foxy up into his arms, scratching her behind her ears. *The way to a cat's heart. And Martha does spoil you.*

She spoils you, too, and you know it, said Foxy.

Ty laughed. *She sure does. OK, I'm going to grab a few changes of clothes, and we'll be off. We need to stop and talk with Jeb, and I'd really like to find Miranda as well.*

Foxy stared at the opening to the cave. *Look no farther. It seems Miranda has found us.*

Ty grabbed his bag with his change of clothes and headed toward Miranda. *Miranda, I need your help.*

The beautiful red fox said, *Rupert told me what happened, and he asked me to help out. He's reported to King Bertram, and he and Samantha are headed back here as quickly as they can.*

OK then, said Ty. *Let's head out.*

Foxy jumped up on Ty's shoulder, and the three of them headed to Dragonwind. They stopped on the outskirts of the village, by a cabin on the edge of the forest, and Ty called out, "Jeb, are you here?"

Jeb came around from the back of his cabin. "Yes, right here. Do you need me?"

"I sure do," said Ty. "We have a situation."

Ty proceeded to explain all that had happened in the last few days. "Are you able to help guard Esme?"

"I certainly am," answered Jeb without a moment's hesitation. "You know what I think about blackmailers, and the only thing worse than them are child abusers. Whatever I can do, I'm here to help."

When they got back to Martha's, Ty found dinner waiting for them all. Martha welcomed everyone. "Come, eat. Kyle is sitting with Esme, and when we're done, I'll go back to sit with her so that he can eat."

They feasted on the wonderful stew Martha had prepared. As they were finishing, Ty said, "Jeb and I will keep watch outside, alternating who's sleeping. Miranda, if you can help us after you meet Esme, that would be great."

Miranda nodded. *Sounds like a plan.*

Ty said, "Thanks, and Foxy, I'd love for you to stay curled up next to Esme. I think she needs all the loving we can give her."

I'm great at that, answered Foxy, getting those who could hear her thoughts to chuckle.

Martha took Jeb, Miranda, and Foxy into Esme's room. Kyle looked up as they entered, and he shook his head to indicate that there had been no change in Esme's condition.

Miranda went over to the bed and nudged Esme's hand. Foxy carefully jumped up on the bed and moved over to curl up next to Esme's right shoulder. Jeb looked at Esme with a horrified expression on his face. "She's thirteen? She looks no more than eight or nine, and she's so thin. She looks so helpless and vulnerable."

Martha put a hand on Jeb's shoulder. "I know. We've really got to give her a lot of love and help. I don't think I've ever seen anyone who's been so badly abused and tortured. She has old wounds and scars going back for years."

"How could anyone do such a thing?" said Jeb.

"She's got some magical abilities," said Martha. "Ty was explaining that to us. Her parents used her for their own financial gain, and somehow this guy The Wraith got word of her and forced her parents to get even more information from her. She has resisted more than I would have thought possible for one so young."

Jeb looked uncomfortable. "I couldn't resist like that. I gave up Ty's secrets with a lot less torture than she's endured."

Martha turned to him so that she could look into his eyes. "Each of us is different. I'm not sure why Esme has the inner strength that she obviously does, but it's the only reason she's still alive. Pain affects each of us differently, and you've stood by Ty for a lot of years. Being burned repeatedly with a cigarette is something I don't think I could have withstood. I know Ty doesn't think any less of you. You are still his best friend and always have been."

"Thanks, Martha," said Jeb. He looked down at Esme again. "I'd better get out to Ty. I'm going to do whatever it takes to protect this young lady."

The first night passed peacefully. Martha and Kyle took turns sitting with Esme. Foxy stayed right next to Esme. Ty, Jeb, and Miranda patrolled the outside.

As dawn broke, Martha heard someone knocking on her front door. She went to answer it and found a group of women standing in front of her home. Sara, one of Martha's oldest friends, said, "We've heard you have a badly injured girl to take care of. We'd like to help. Can we keep your bakery going for you while you take care of her? All of us," she continued as she waved at the group, "know how to bake, and maybe the bread and rolls won't be quite as good as yours, but at least we can keep folks supplied and take that worry off your hands."

Martha's jaw dropped in surprise. "How did you know?" she stammered.

Sara laughed. "News travels fast in a village. Now, will you let us help?"

Martha looked at the group, and after taking a deep breath, she said, "I would be honored to have your assistance. I'll go unlock the bakery front door. Meet you there, and thank you so much."

Martha went back inside to grab her keys. The bakery adjoined her cottage, but it had its own entrance. She let the women in and explained to Sara where the list of special orders was kept. Sara and the women got right to work. Martha just stood there, dumbfounded, until Sara noticed, went over to her friend, gave her a hug, and then said, "Leave this all to us. You go help that poor girl."

Martha left the women to it and went back to her cottage, where she found Ty waiting to hear what had happened.

"Sara and the others are going to keep the bakery going. They knew all about our situation. So much for keeping it secret."

Ty looked worried, but then he smiled. "We really should have known. There are no secrets in a small village."

The day passed quietly, and there was no change in Esme until evening. She was still unconscious and unresponsive, but by nightfall she began running a fever. Martha called Ty inside as Esme's fever became alarmingly high.

"I don't know how to treat this," said Martha. "I've been dripping a feverwort compound as often as I dare. She has swallowed some, but her fever is still rising. Can you help her?"

"I'll try," said Ty. "I've so far been unable to make telepathic contact with her, but now she's getting really restless. Maybe I can reach her."

Ty sat on one side of Esme's bed and Martha on the other. Martha kept cool, damp cloths on Esme's forehead as Ty worked. Esme was in great distress, and Ty tried to probe her mind telepathically, sending loving and reassuring thoughts.

It took him a long time to get anything, but when he did, he nearly recoiled in horror. Esme was reliving her abuse—her beatings, her whippings, her starvation. Ty put a hand on her arm and tried to comfort her, but she couldn't be calmed.

Martha and Ty worked tirelessly all night long. By dawn, they were afraid they were losing her. It was so sad, but Esme's strength, which had always been more strength of mind than strength of body, was failing.

They were discussing what else they could do when Rupert and Samantha rushed into the room. Ty looked up. *How did you two get here so quickly?*

We've been running night and day, said Rupert breathlessly. *I could tell Esme was failing, and I had to get here.*

Rupert went right over to Esme, and he jumped carefully onto the bed and licked her face. *Esme, it's Rupert. Please, I'm here now. Come back to me.*

Ty moved aside to give Rupert more room as Rupert took over the telepathic communications. Ty switched to his healing magic instead, trying desperately to bolster Esme's strength.

Rupert entered what seemed to be a trancelike state. Ty and Martha were quiet as Rupert worked for hours. Then Rupert all but collapsed, and Martha said, "Rupert, when did you and Samantha last eat?"

Rupert didn't answer, but Martha wasn't fooled. She stepped to the doorway and called out to Kyle, "We need two bowls of stew here for some very weary travelers."

Kyle arrived in just a few minutes and handed Martha the two bowls. Martha gave one to Samantha and then handed Rupert's bowl to Ty. Ty held Rupert and gently placed the bowl within reach. Ty dipped his finger into the bowl and gently rubbed it on Rupert's gums. Immediately Rupert licked his lips and soon was devouring Martha's stew.

Thank you, said Rupert when he finished. *That helped a lot. Ty, she's very weak. And she's in a really dark place. She feels so helpless, and she's reliving all her pain. If that weren't bad enough, she's also blaming herself for all the times she broke down and gave her parents information that they then used themselves or passed on to The Wraith. I've been trying to let her know that she's been extremely brave and that she's held out longer than most adults would, but she sees only her failures. That's weakening her faster than I can stop.*

Ty thought for a while. *Did you and Esme ever have any fun? Did you ever tell stories or laugh? I know her life has been brutally horrible, but were there ever any happier moments?*

Rupert pondered this for a few moments. *One day I brought her a doll that Queen Elicia gave me. Esme loved that doll, and we talked a lot about how Esme would build her a house. Unfortunately, her parents found the doll and destroyed it.*

Can you remind her of the joy she felt when she got the doll? asked Ty. *Can you try to find other good times? Even fleeting ones? We need to find a way to give her hope.*

Rupert went back into a trance state with Esme, trying to remember all the positives that he could. Meanwhile, Ty sent healing energies to both Esme and Rupert. Instinctively he knew that Rupert was Esme's only hope.

The day passed with no visible changes. Martha kept dripping her feverwort infusion into Esme and bathing her forehead with cool cloths. Ty kept up his magical healing efforts. Foxy stayed close to Esme, giving the comfort that only a cat can. Kyle brought food and water for everyone at regular intervals. Jeb and Miranda kept watch outside. Everyone was exhausted and extremely stressed. It seemed that in spite of their best efforts, Esme was fading before their eyes.

Samantha began to sing very softly in her squirrel chirping voice. She sat on the head of the bed, watching Esme. As Samantha sang, Rupert hummed. There was no change in Esme at first, but as their voices grew stronger, Esme grew less restless. Ty said softly, *Keep singing.*

Samantha and Rupert did just that, and as they did so, Ty monitored Esme's thoughts. He finally found what he was looking for: a positive thought. Ty told Rupert, *She's remembering a summer day when she sang with you and Samantha. You were on her window ledge so she could touch you. That's the kind of memory we need to strengthen.*

I didn't realize she liked it, said Samantha. *Squirrels aren't known for their singing.*

Ty chuckled. *What she's valuing is your friendship. In her dark world, you and Rupert were her only hope for something better. And face it, she wouldn't have escaped without you both. So sing on! Strengthen the bond of love between you and her.*

Another night passed, and while Esme was slightly less restless, her fever was still too high. Martha debated putting her in a tub of cold water to try to bring the fever down, but she was afraid that might be too big a shock for her. Martha continued the warm compresses on the arrow wound to try to pull out the last of the infection there. They just kept doing what they were doing and hoped it would be enough.

Samantha's and Rupert's voices tired, so they alternated singing, one at a time, so that the other could rest. Ty took breaks every couple of hours to go outside and check on Jeb and Miranda and be sure everything was quiet. Healing magic was tiring work, and he really needed to sleep, but he was afraid they might lose Esme if they didn't all keep doing their parts, so instead he made himself a sandwich and then went back to the sickroom.

As dawn broke, Martha reported that Esme's fever was down slightly. She hoped that meant that the worst was over. However, she was very concerned that Esme hadn't had anything to eat and very little to drink in over a week. There wasn't a lot they could do about that as long as Esme was unconscious, but Martha kept dribbling small quantities of her herbal remedies and vegetable broth into Esme.

Later that morning, Rupert said, *Esme's not in such a dark place. Her nightmares have lessened. I keep talking to her, and for the first time since she was injured, I think she's hearing me. I can't be positive. It's just a feeling I have.*

Samantha said, *I agree. I think Esme is surfacing.*

Esme's fever continued to drop as the day wore on. By nightfall, her sleep seemed much more natural. Martha and Ty went to get some rest, Martha in her bedroom and Ty on the living room couch, as long as Rupert, Samantha, and Kyle promised to call them if there was any change in Esme's condition.

Ty woke up the next morning to the sound of Martha's call. "Ty, come quick."

Ty went into the sickroom and found that Esme was finally awake. Ty smiled. "I expect you don't remember me, but you're now safe, and we're so glad you're awake. You've had us really worried."

Esme, who had her arms wrapped around Rupert, looked at Ty. "Who are you?"

Ty explained all that had happened since Esme's father had attacked. The last thing Esme remembered was falling off the cliff. When Ty told her that a dragon had flown her to Dragonwind, Esme gasped. "I was helped by a dragon and I missed that?"

Ty laughed. "You just get well, and Criseda and I will be happy to give you a ride."

Martha had a bowl of broth ready for Esme, and after Ty helped Esme to sit up a bit, Martha fed her. Kyle came into the room, and Ty noticed that Esme's first reaction was one of alarm, but that quickly subsided, and she smiled as Kyle introduced himself.

Ty asked, "Esme, can you tell me a bit about your magical gift? I suspect it's more than just being telepathic."

Esme hesitated and then said, "I know what people are thinking. And more than that, I have an inner sense as to whether they are good or whether they mean harm."

Kyle smiled. "That's a really useful gift to have."

Esme frowned. "Not if others want to use the gift for their own evil purposes."

Ty said very gently, "We can all see just how much you've been through, Esme, and how badly you've been treated. We've all sworn to protect you. Your gift is unique, and even without it, you are a special person. We're going to see that you get to have a good life now, doing whatever you want to do, becoming your own person."

Tears streamed down Esme's face. Martha gave her a handkerchief and then said, "You need to rest now. What you need is lots of rest and lots of food, and that's what we're going to concentrate on for now."

"Can Rupert and Samantha stay with me?" asked Esme.

"Of course," said Ty, "and this lovely black cat is Foxy. She'd like to stay with you also, if that's OK with you."

Esme moved her left hand from Rupert to Foxy and stroked her back. "She's so soft."

Ty smiled. "That she is. She's a very good friend. You rest now, and when you next wake up, we'll have you meet Miranda, another wonderful fox and a good friend of Rupert's, as well as my best friend, Jeb. They've been guarding the house."

As Ty made this last statement, Esme grabbed for Rupert as a look of terror crossed her face. Ty quickly added, "Don't worry. We're just being extra careful. No one is going to hurt you while you're under our care. Just remember, your only job now is to get well and strong."

With that, Kyle and Ty left the room, and Martha settled Esme comfortably under the covers before joining them in the kitchen.

Kyle was the first to speak. "That young lady is terrified, and her only true security is the friendship of Rupert and Samantha. It's going to be a while before she can truly trust and heal."

Ty nodded. "I agree, but her ability to sense people's true intentions will help her a lot, I imagine."

"Well, I'm going to work on getting some meat on her bones," said Martha, "as well as getting her some exercise, once that leg heals."

"How are the ladies doing with your bakery?" asked Ty.

"They've been amazing," said Martha. "I've asked them to keep on for another day so that I can be sure Esme doesn't have a relapse, but then I should be able to leave her in Rupert, Foxy, and Samantha's care long enough to do my baking."

Jeb stuck his head in through the kitchen door. "I hear Esme's awake."

Ty laughed. "Well, she was, but she's napping now. Next time she's awake, we'll introduce you. How are you holding up?"

"Fine," said Jeb. "Miranda and I have traded four-hour shifts, but I'll admit, I'll be glad when you and Kyle can help out, not that you haven't been really busy as well."

"As Martha said to her friends who are keeping the bakery running, let's keep the status quo for another day to be sure Esme's over the worst of her injuries, and then we'll make a new plan that involves sleep for everyone, I promise," said Ty.

CHAPTER 5

HEALING

Over the next week, Esme made rapid progress, eating Martha's delicious foods, napping, and enjoying the company of Rupert, Samantha, and Foxy. She still was confined to her bed because of the broken leg, but the arrow wound in the other leg was nearly healed, thanks to Martha's poultices and Ty's healing magic. Her ribs were healed as well, and her headache was nearly gone.

The result of all the healing was that she was getting a bit bored, not being able to do anything. Martha asked, "Do you like to read? I could get you some books if you like."

Esme looked embarrassed and finally said, "I don't know how to read. I've tried to teach myself, but my parents found the one book I'd managed to get and they were furious."

Martha looked shocked. "But you went to school, didn't you?"

"No," said Esme sadly. "I was never allowed that either. They couldn't take a chance that I'd tell someone what they were doing to me. They told the school I was being homeschooled, and they sent in false reports, but I never got any lessons."

"But they got you to read people's minds so they could blackmail them. You had to have seen those people in order to read their minds, didn't you?"

"Not once my parents realized that I could read minds at a distance of about twenty paces. After that, they just brought people over or had conversations near my window. I, of course, was threatened with the worst punishments if I even let on I was in the house."

Martha was silent, trying to digest all this. Finally, she said, "Would you like to learn to read and write?"

"Oh yes, please," said Esme.

Martha nodded. "I have a good friend, Elfrida, who is a retired school-teacher. I'll go check with her to see if she'd be willing to teach you."

"Thank you," said Esme in a soft voice.

Martha left the room and went in search of Ty. "We have a problem. I just found out that Esme has never been to school. She doesn't know how to read or write. Heaven knows what else she's never been taught, but we have our work cut out for us."

Ty looked as shocked as Martha had when she'd heard. "What can we do?"

"I'm going to go see Elfrida right now. I'm sure she'll want to teach Esme. Esme is so sweet, and she really wants to learn."

"That's a great idea, and it will give Esme something to concentrate on while her leg is healing."

That afternoon, Martha introduced Esme to Elfrida, a small, white-haired lady with penetrating blue eyes and a smile that crinkled her face in kindly wrinkles.

Esme was obviously taken with Elfrida, who arrived with a selection of books with animal stories in them. She also had a slate tablet for writing. "I understand that you've been denied an education. I'm here to get you caught up, and we're going to have a grand time while we do that."

Esme gave Elfrida a shy smile. "I'd like that. I managed to teach myself the letters and simple words from a beginning reader Samantha got for me. Rupert and Samantha helped me, and we were doing OK until…"

Elfrida patted Esme on the hand. "I know, dear. Martha told me. But now, you can learn just as much as you want to. Rupert, Samantha, Foxy, you can learn too if you wish."

With that, the lessons began. Elfrida came every afternoon for four hours, and the time seemed to fly by for both Esme and Elfrida. Elfrida also assigned Esme homework to do in the mornings before lessons resumed. As Elfrida was leaving one day after two weeks of lessons, she stopped in the kitchen to talk with Ty and Martha. "That child is really smart. I guess she'd have to be to have survived as well as she has. She's now reading at about a nine- or ten-year-old's level. We've added in math, and she loves to draw, as you've no doubt seen. I should have her caught up to where she ought to be in maybe another month. Do you plan to enroll her in the village school?"

Ty looked at Martha before he spoke. "I don't think that would be in Esme's best interests. She's still really skittish around others, and she'd be an easy target for teasing or bullying. Her psychological damage has to be intense, and we have to be careful not to trigger anything."

"I understand," said Elfrida. "To be honest, she's too bright for a regular classroom anyway. Just look at how quickly she's picked up on things so far."

Martha smiled at her friend. "You're looking great as well. I think having a bright student is giving you new energies."

Elfrida nodded. "You're right there. I've really missed teaching, but I'm not up to handling a classroom full of students. But one on one with someone who wants to learn, well, that couldn't be better. I can't believe what her parents did to her."

"I'm going to head to the palace tomorrow to talk with King Bertram, but I'm betting we haven't heard the last of them. After all, she still is underage," said Ty. "I'm sure King Bertram will grant guardianship of Esme to Martha, but I need to get that paperwork done."

"We'll keep her safe while you're gone," said Martha.

"I've talked with both Kyle and Jeb, and they're confident they can keep guard with Miranda's help, and I can leave early in the morning, riding White Star, and hopefully be back late tomorrow night," said Ty.

True to his word, Ty and White Star were on the road headed to the capital before the sun was up. White Star was eager for a fast run, and Ty realized that, with all his time taken up protecting Esme, he'd been neglecting his beloved horse. The two of them enjoyed their fast ride down through the mountains and across the plains. They arrived at the palace just as King Bertram and his family were finishing breakfast.

"Ty," said Queen Elicia, "please have a seat, and I'll have some breakfast brought in for you."

"Thanks," said Ty as he ruffled nine-year-old Lance's hair; kissed the three-year-old twins, Harriet and Hazel, on their cheeks; and shook hands with Raymond, King Bertram's eldest, and Malcolm, King Bertram's nephew and foster son, both of whom were fifteen years old. As he passed Queen Elicia, he kissed her on the cheek and then gave a playful poke in the chest to six-month-old Ernest, who was intent on spreading oatmeal everywhere. Then he grabbed a nearby chair and sat down.

Queen Elicia stood, picked up Ernest, and said to the rest of the children, "Time for lessons. Ty, will we see you later?"

"Yes, for a bit. White Star and I do have to get back to Dragonwind tonight, but I can stay until after lunch if that's convenient."

"Yeah!" yelled the twins.

Lance said, "I want to show you what I've built."

"You can't hog him," said Raymond.

Ty held up his hands. "If you let me talk to your father, then I'll have time for all of you before I go, I promise."

With that, the queen and the children left the room.

King Bertram chuckled. "They sure do love it when you visit." Then he became serious. "How's Esme?"

As he ate, Ty brought him up to date on the current events in Dragonwind. "None of us could believe that Esme had never gotten to go to school. What that poor girl has been through is beyond horrible."

"I agree," said Bertram, "and I've been doing some research on my end as well. Do you remember Lord Plumfield?"

"He was one of Lord Osterfels's hunting cronies, wasn't he, from a neighboring kingdom?"

"Yes, he was part of the group that was supposed to help Lord Osterfels overthrow me, but when you caught Lord Osterfels and exposed his plots as well as his responsibility for the murder of your parents, they just faded away. However, I have some suspicions that Lord Plumfield didn't fade as far away as we might have thought."

"What's going on?" asked Ty.

"I've not got a lot to go on, but I think at least two members of my council of advisers are in contact with him. And they haven't let me know anything about it."

"Which two?" asked Ty.

"Lord Upworth and Lord Gofrond," said Bertram.

"Lord Upworth has lands near Dragonwind. He does a lot of mining, and I've heard disquieting rumors about how he does that mining," said Ty.

"And Lord Gofrond's lands are on the border, next to Lord Plumfield's," said the king.

"OK, we definitely need more information. I can begin with Lord Upworth, if you want, as he's closest to me and I don't want to leave Esme unprotected," said Ty.

"Start there, and if you need more help protecting Esme, just let me know," said the king.

"For starters," said Ty, "I need a legal document granting Esme's guardianship to Martha. She's only thirteen and so technically under her parents' control. Their rights to her need to be revoked."

"Of course," said the king as he stood. "Come into my office, and I'll give you some documents, including Esme's new guardianship papers. I also want to officially appoint you as my roving ambassador, with authority to make arrests and call for assistance from village militia."

The two men walked down the hallway to King Bertram's office, and Bertram motioned Ty to a chair while he went around to his desk and began pulling out parchment, quills, ink, and his royal seal. Ty waited as the king wrote out two documents, signed them, and sealed them with his red seal before putting them into a courier pouch and handing that to Ty.

Bertram then said, "Is there anything else? Any ideas about The Wraith?"

"Honestly, I haven't given it as much thought as I would have liked," admitted Ty. "At first we weren't sure that Esme would even live, so our efforts were entirely focused on not losing her."

"Understandable," said Bertram.

"And thank you for sending Rupert and Samantha back so quickly," said Ty. "I think we would have lost her without them, especially Rupert. Esme is traumatized, and she won't let Rupert out of her sight except for his necessary trips outside, and when he's doing that, she's borderline panicked even though he makes his trips as short as possible."

"That poor young girl," said Bertram.

"But if the rumors I've heard are true, there could be more kids like Esme out there, maybe not with her magical gifts, but being used as slave labor. We have to stop him, whoever he is."

"Agreed," said Bertram. "Several of the other foxes who live near the palace have agreed to keep the fox communication network going in Rupert's absence, so you can send messages through Miranda and they'll reach me."

"Good to know," said Ty as both men stood and left the office.

The rest of the morning was spent with King Bertram and Queen Elicia's children. Ty allowed himself to be tugged this way and that, so he spent time with each and every one of them, praising their projects. He was pleased to see how well Malcolm fit into his uncle's family, and both Bertram and Elicia made sure he was included just the way their children were. Malcolm had been hit hard by the treason of his father and twin brother, as well as his own and his mother's near murders. King Bertram had set up Malcolm's mother in her own cottage on the palace grounds, and both of them were doing well now. Ty could only hope that Esme's path would end in such a good place.

Lunch was a loud, happy affair with the six children vying for Ty's attention. Ernest wanted Ty to feed him, which Ty found to be a challenging adventure. The other five talked over one another, telling Ty of their exploits. Bertram and Elicia looked fondly at their charges. Ty found himself relaxing for the first time in weeks, just enjoying the hubbub.

Finally, when the youngest children had been put down for afternoon naps and the older ones sent off for their afternoon lessons, Ty said farewell to Elicia and Bertram, thanking them for a lovely visit and promising Bertram more information as soon as he had it. He and White Star then made the return trip to Dragonwind, happy to reach Martha's and find that all was well and that there had been no trouble.

CHAPTER 6

NIGHTMARES

That night, the entire household was awakened by screams from Esme. Rupert tried to calm her, but she was in the throes of a horrible nightmare. She'd had them before, sometimes several times in one night, but she hadn't had one in a few weeks.

Ty gently woke Esme, who grabbed him fiercely as if her life depended on it and said, "He's coming; I know he is."

"Who?" asked Ty. "Your father?"

"Yes," said Esme. "This time I'm really sure. I know I've said that before, but this time is different. It was very real."

Ty kept his arms wrapped around her, and Martha came in bearing a mug of chamomile tea. Esme sipped the tea, thanking Martha. Ty stood up, giving Martha his seat, and said, "I'm going to check outside with Jeb, Kyle, and Miranda. Don't worry. We'll keep you safe."

Rupert put his head in Esme's lap, and Samantha and Foxy snuggled closer to her as well. Martha looked at Ty. "Be careful out there."

Ty nodded and left. Outside he found everything to be secure. The watchers hadn't spotted any disturbances, but Miranda said, *I think you told me that Esme can sense people from a distance of what, twenty or thirty feet?*

Ty spoke aloud so that Jeb would be included in Ty's side of the conversations. "Yes, and maybe a greater distance for those she knows well, possibly up to fifty feet. We've never tested it."

Jeb said, "We've not seen anyone new in the village. I've tried searching down the trail toward the capital, but I've not seen any traces of anyone."

Kyle nodded in agreement. "Nothing seems to have changed that we can see."

"Well, it could be just another nightmare," said Ty. "Certainly she's more than entitled to those after all she's been through. Nevertheless, I don't want to make any assumptions."

A lovely brown rabbit hopped into the yard, and Ty said, "Hi, Mirabella. Do you have information for us?"

No, the rabbit answered, *but I do have an idea. I know you don't want to add more people to Esme's watch, but how would it be if Miranda and I brought in more forest friends? We wouldn't be noticed by any humans, or at least not thought of as a threat. We can go farther afield and hence give you more warning if we do find anyone.*

Ty slapped the side of his head. "Why didn't we think of that? You're brilliant, Mirabella. You and your friends could search for several miles in all directions, couldn't you?"

Definitely, said Mirabella.

And we can use the fox communication network to send information back to you, added Miranda.

"I think that's an excellent idea," said Ty, and Jeb and Kyle agreed, once Ty explained Miranda's plan. "How soon can you get your friends to start the search?"

Mirabella seemed to give a low chuckle before saying, *They're already heading out. We figured you'd like the plan.*

"Great," said Ty. "I'll let Esme know. Maybe that will calm her enough so that she can sleep."

Ty went back inside and reported on the new plan. Esme said, "They won't be hurt, will they?"

"No," said Ty. "They won't try to attack anyone. They'll just watch and then alert us if they see anyone coming our way. They'll be safe, and you should be able to relax and get back to sleep."

Esme nodded and slid down under her covers. Rupert, Foxy, and Samantha crowded around her, and Martha and Ty left so that she could get some sleep.

In the kitchen, Martha said, "Do you really think her father is coming?"

Ty shrugged his shoulders. "I don't know, but we can't take any chances. Her parents aren't very bright, but they're greedy, and they obviously have no qualms about hurting her. On top of that, they've made themselves minions of The Wraith, and I'm very sure that The Wraith isn't going to give up on Esme. Her magical talents are too strong for him to pass them by."

Martha nodded. "We still have a few hours before dawn. I think we should both try to get some sleep."

Ty agreed, and they headed to their respective beds. Ty missed his cave, and Martha's couch wasn't long enough for him, but he wasn't going to leave Esme. A less-than-ideal bed was a small price to pay for her safety.

Things remained calm for the next week, and Martha decided that Esme's broken leg was healed sufficiently to remove the splints. Esme was overjoyed to be able to move around a bit, but Martha told her she needed to be very careful and take things slowly. Martha worked with her to show her how to strengthen her leg, how to start bending it a little at a time, and how to take care of it. Best of all, Esme could now have a real bath, something she'd never had before in her captivity, and she was thrilled with the sweet-smelling bubbles that Martha added to the bathwater. Her shrieks of joy rang through the house as she bathed in the tub Martha had set up in the kitchen, and the others smiled to hear her so happy. Esme wanted to take Rupert, Samantha, and Foxy into the tub with her, but all three of her friends quickly declined and moved as far away from the tub as they could and still be in the kitchen.

When Elfrida arrived that day for afternoon lessons, she was pleased to see that Esme was sitting at the kitchen table, and Esme had to tell her all about the bubble bath. Elfrida smiled. "Why don't you write a story about it?"

Esme thought about it for a moment. "In my story, can I get Rupert into the bath?"

Elfrida laughed. "It's your story. You can put anyone in it anywhere you want."

Esme said, "I don't think Rupert would mind being in a story about a bath."

With that, Esme grabbed her writing supplies and set to work.

The next morning, Ty noticed a couple of vultures in a nearby tree. He remembered what Rupert and Samantha had told him about the vultures appearing before the attack on the road, so he told Miranda, Kyle, and Jeb to be extra vigilant.

Three hours later, Miranda reported, *A group of about twenty men is headed this way. The leader seems to be Esme's father. They look very angry.*

"Thanks, Miranda," said Ty. "How long before they get here?"

Mirabella estimates about an hour, maybe a little more.

Ty turned to Jeb and Kyle. "Gather any men whom you can trust. I'm going to call to Criseda to see if she can help us. She'll need to get permission from either Magnolia or Sapphire, as this would be against their normal protocol, but I believe they might think Esme's fate is important to the planet as a whole—at least I hope so."

"Good luck," said Kyle as he and Jeb headed to find those willing to defend the village.

Ty called to Criseda. *We have a party of armed men headed to Dragonwind to take Esme back. The king has given her guardianship to Martha, but somehow I don't think they're going to care about that.*

I'm sorry, Ty, but we can't interfere in the running of human affairs, said Criseda. *I wish I could.*

I know, said Ty. *But Esme's magic is something really unique. You know better than I do that very few humans have magic. I know of only three of us. King Bertram has a weak telepathic ability; I have telepathic and healing magic; but Esme's ability to read minds, communicate telepathically, and, more than that, to sense the true nature of people—what's truly in their hearts—is something hitherto unknown. And if The Wraith gets ahold of her, you know he'll use her not only to destroy us but also to do whatever he wants with the planet as a whole. Can't you get some kind of agreement with your fellow dragons so that you can scare these guys off, at least?*

You make a good point, said Criseda. *Let me try. I'll get back to you as quickly as I can.*

Ty went into Martha's cottage to get Martha and Esme. He wanted them to leave and go to his cave.

Esme started crying when she heard that her father was on the way. She picked up Samantha and hugged her. Rupert jumped into her lap.

Martha said, "Ty, we'd never get there. We're safer here in the village. Our friends will help, I'm sure of it."

Ty wasn't sure what to do. Then he looked out the front window and saw that the yard was filling up with woodland creatures. Kyle and Jeb were heading back to the cottage at the head of about thirty village men. Maybe they would be able to defend and protect Esme.

Ty, called Criseda, *I've been told I can't do anything but that I can fly over the village and even sit on Martha's roof.*

Ty smiled. *That will help a lot.*

Ty went outside to talk to the men. "I'm sure by now everyone knows just how badly Esme was abused by her parents," he began. "I've been to King Bertram, and he's given guardianship of Esme to Martha, so we're here to see that Esme is protected from her abusers. If these men listen and go away, then we won't need to act, but if they try force, we'll stop them."

Ty was pleased to see the determined look on the villagers' faces. He divided them into groups and positioned them around Martha's cottage. He set Kyle and Jeb in the rear because he was afraid that someone might try a sneak attack at the back while everyone was distracted by the goings-on in the front.

Once everyone was in position, they didn't have long to wait. Soon Stephen and his thugs walked into the village, and when they spotted Ty, they headed over to the front of Martha's cottage.

Stephen waved his bow and arrow. "I'm here for my daughter. Hand her over."

Ty looked him directly in the eyes. "You have no more rights to her. King Bertram has given Martha guardianship of Esme in this village and renounced your claims to her because you abused her so badly."

"I didn't abuse her," said Stephen.

One of the village women spoke up. "We saw her when she first came here. She'd been badly beaten, and she was starving, her ribs sticking out of her chest, no muscles. No child should ever look like that."

"Shut up, you stupid woman," said Stephen. "She's my child, and I can discipline her as I think she needs. That's nobody else's business."

"Yes, actually it is," said Ty. "You haven't allowed her to go to school. You've kept her locked up in a tiny room. She's malnourished, and her physical development is that of someone much younger. That's all illegal, and King Bertram has signed the custody order. You and your men have made a wasted trip. Please leave now."

"I'm not going without Esme," snarled Stephen.

"Oh, but you are," said Ty.

"Take 'em," shouted Stephen, lifting his bow and preparing to shoot.

Several of the other men did the same, but the villagers were prepared and they shot first, hitting Stephen's men in their arms and legs. They were trying not to kill anyone. The woodland creatures stepped forward and began latching onto legs with their teeth. A couple of skunks turned and sprayed the group, which proved to be one of the most effective weapons. Then Criseda swooped down low over the group before taking up a position on Martha's roof. She let out a roar of flames, which she directed up into the sky so that it wouldn't hurt anyone, but that was more than most of Stephen's men could take.

As Stephen's men turned and ran or hobbled out of the village, Stephen said, "You haven't seen the last of me."

"I hope for your sake that we have," said Ty.

CHAPTER 7

New Friends

Ty was sure they hadn't seen the last of Stephen and his thugs, but he was feeling very good about the watchfulness of the forest creatures, and he really wanted to give Esme a more normal life, so he moved back home, although he came into Dragonwind each day. Jeb went back to his work as the forest guardian.

Martha worked in the bakery, and now that Esme was healed, she began teaching her to bake. They worked in the mornings, then Esme had her lessons with Elfrida in the afternoons, and in the evenings, Esme did her homework. Kyle did odd chores in the village, unless Martha needed assistance, and he made sure to keep an ear out for any trouble.

Ty and Kyle had been very pleased with the way the villagers had rallied to defend Esme, but they also knew that Ty still had some enemies in the village, those who hadn't understood his transgendered nature and who resented the fact that thanks to the dragons, he now had a body that matched his true identity.

Most of the villagers had finally accepted Ty as a genuinely kind person who helped any in need, and they didn't worry about anything else. The fact that Ty had healing magic, which he shared with any who asked, helped them to see Ty's true nature. Ty's friendship with Criseda was thought odd, but as long as the dragon left them alone, they were willing to accept her flying overhead. After her appearance when Stephen and his thugs were threatening, the village started to take pride in being protected by a dragon. They felt that the name of their village was well deserved.

But while most of the village interactions were very positive, Ty knew that it was still possible that there could be those who were under the thumb of The Wraith, whoever he was. So Ty and Kyle listened and kept watch.

Esme loved her work in the bakery. She made friends with Martha's friend Sara, who had so enjoyed her time in the bakery when Martha was nursing Esme that she'd stayed on as Martha's assistant baker. Esme felt very comfortable with both women, and she was learning fast. Her arms weren't yet strong enough to knead bread dough, but she was very good at making chocolate chip cookies and brownies.

"Can I put some raisins in the oatmeal cookies?" Esme asked. "I love raisins."

Martha chuckled. "That's a very good idea. You may even use the raisins to make faces on the cookies if you want."

Esme smiled. "I'll make happy faces."

The only thing Esme didn't want to do was work out in the front of the shop where the customers came in, and Martha understood that. Martha didn't want to expose Esme to more people than she had to. The villagers didn't know about Esme's magic, and Martha wanted to keep it that way.

When the bell over the store's front door jangled to indicate a customer, either Martha or Sara would go out into the shop. One day when this happened, Esme grabbed Martha's arm and said, "I think someone out there is going to try to steal from you."

Martha looked surprised but nodded. She went out into the store and saw a mother with a boy who looked to be about ten years old. The mother smiled and asked, "Do you have any day-old bread for sale?"

Martha showed her the bin where she put her sale items, and the woman said, "I'll take three loaves."

As Martha put the order in a bag, she saw, out of the corner of her eye, that the boy had slipped another loaf under his coat as the mother tried to distract Martha with another question. Martha wasn't sure she would have noticed if Esme hadn't alerted her ahead of time, as the boy was really quick.

Martha handed the bag to the woman and said, "So four loaves of day-old bread. Is that all?"

The woman said, "No, it's three loaves."

Martha just smiled and looked at the boy. "Four loaves. Three in this bag and one under his coat."

"Well, I never," said the woman. "Are you calling us thieves?"

"No," said Martha. "I'm just charging for what you asked for or already took. If you only want three loaves, then I'll take back one from this bag."

The woman slapped the boy across his face. "You got caught. There will be a price to pay for that when you get home."

Martha collected the money and then turned to the woman. "I'd prefer it if you didn't shop here again. I don't know where you're from. You're not a resident of Dragonwind. You'll find that we are honest, hardworking folk who don't appreciate thieves. If you need food and can't afford it, we'll always help, but we don't condone stealing. Have a good day."

The woman started to argue, but after she took one look at Martha's face, she just turned, grabbed her son by his arm, and left the shop, slamming the door as she went.

Martha went into the back and gave Esme a hug. "Thank you, Esme."

Sara said, "How did you know, Esme?"

Esme looked at Martha. "I don't know. I just did."

"We need to tell Ty," said Martha. "Those two don't live in Dragonwind, and it really looked as if the mother was taking advantage of her son's ability to steal. They could be working under The Wraith."

Esme started to tremble, and Martha drew her into a hug. "I don't know this, Esme. They could just be very poor, down on their luck, and living on the road. I just think Ty needs to know."

Sara said, "I've noticed a few strangers heading along the road between us and the capital. I'm not sure where they've come from, maybe from the mining villages northeast of us. I've heard rumors that the mines aren't producing the way they used to."

Martha didn't get a chance to talk privately with Ty until after dinner, but when she finally did, he said, "I've heard the same rumors. I need to check out Lord Upworth, who has mines in the area. He's one of King Bertram's advisers. When I'm there, I'll see what I can find out about the mines and who's working them."

Esme came in then and said, "That woman and her son, the ones in the bakery, they were really scared. I think they were being forced to steal, but I couldn't tell who was making them. I didn't get any feeling that it was The Wraith. I think maybe Martha was right that they were just having a hard time."

"Thanks, Esme," said Ty. "And thank you for alerting Martha. We'll know a lot more about what's going on with your help."

Esme went off to do her homework, and Ty said, "I don't want Esme ever left on her own."

"I agree," said Martha. "When I mentioned the possibility that that woman was working for The Wraith, Esme turned as white as a sheet. And if she came across someone who had intentions to do harm, rather than just steal some bread, she might not know how to protect herself."

"I think it would be good to ask Jeb if he'd teach her some defensive strategies, how to defend herself if someone tries to attack her," said Ty. "I'll talk to him tomorrow about setting up a time to do that."

Martha said, "That would be good. And although I'm not sure that everyone would want to know that we have a fox and a squirrel in the kitchen of the bakery, remember, Esme is never actually alone. Rupert and Samantha are always with her. Did you see Stephen's nose, or what's left of it? I'd say Rupert is a pretty darned good deterrent."

Ty laughed. "For sure. And there are lots more forest friends watching out for Esme now. She's won over a lot of hearts."

Ty headed out of Dragonwind early the next morning, heading toward the cluster of small mining towns. He rode White Star, and the two enjoyed the sunny, cool, crisp autumn day. As he rode, Ty noticed that there was more traffic on the road than he would have expected. There were a few wagons loaded with furniture and family goods, driven by parents with kids. There were some walking along the road, with full packs on their backs. When Ty stopped to inquire where they were going, he was met with a sullen silence. No one, it seemed, wanted to talk. The most common answer was, "We're tired of the mountains and want to live in a less remote area."

Ty could understand that reasoning, but what he couldn't understand was why so many families had decided at the same time to leave, and why they all had children who were six to ten years old. Something was driving these families out of the mining villages, and something had scared them into not talking.

As he neared the first of the small mining villages, he came upon a wagon with a broken rear axle stuck in a ditch. The father was trying to pull the wagon back onto the road, but he wasn't having any luck. Ty got down off White Star and offered assistance. The father looked nervous but finally agreed. Ty put a rope around the front axle and then tied the other end of the rope around the horn on his saddle. He and White Star slowly pulled on the wagon as the father pushed, and between them, they got the wagon back up onto the road.

The father looked at the damaged wagon and then sat down, utterly defeated. There was no way they could repair it. Ty said, "We'll have to fashion a new axle. Is there a blacksmith in your village?"

"Yes," said the man, who finally let Ty know his name was Wilson, "but he's not allowed to do anything that isn't mine related. He wouldn't be allowed to make a new axle for a wagon, especially a wagon that's leaving town."

"Where are you and your family going?" asked Ty.

"We don't know," admitted Wilson, "but we need to get out of here. It isn't safe anymore. And my son is old enough to be taken to work in the mines. My wife and I don't want him in there."

Ty looked at the family. The mother was a small woman with a worried expression. She was holding on to her son, who looked to be about six years old. He was certainly too young to be working in a mine. Ty realized that his trip to the mines would have to wait. He needed to turn around and help this family get to Dragonwind. Ty asked Wilson, "So it's just the three of you?"

"Yes," said Wilson.

"How would it be if you and I, with the help of White Star, pulled your wagon off the road and into the woods over there?" asked Ty, pointing off to the side of the road. "We can do our best to hide the wagon. Pack anything really important, though, and then your wife and son can ride on White Star, and you and I will walk. I'm from Dragonwind, and we can get you at least that far."

Wilson stared hard at Ty. "But why would you do that? You don't even know us. And you were headed toward the mines."

"I help where I can, and truly, I can't see anyone putting a six-year-old into the mines. It's not right," answered Ty. "My business at the mines can wait. Now we'd better get moving before anyone else comes along. Are you willing?"

Wilson looked at his wife, who nodded, and he turned back to Ty. "I'd be most grateful for your help."

It didn't take long to get the wagon hidden, and soon they were on their way again. Ty learned that Wilson's wife's name was Selena, and their son was Ralph. Wilson was a carpenter, but now the only work for him was in the mines. He refused to work there because there were no safety provisions, and mine collapses were a common occurrence. If you didn't work in the mines, then there wasn't any way to support yourself.

Ty assured him that there was always work in Dragonwind for a good carpenter. As they walked, Ty learned more about the conditions in the mining villages. There were four small villages surrounding the mines, and originally they'd been separate, but Lord Upworth bought up all the mines and took over the four villages. Now he ran everything.

Ty thought about this as they walked. He didn't like what he heard, but he knew there were plenty of greedy landowners, and Lord Upworth could run his mines however he liked. But there had to be a way to stop him from using children. Ty just didn't know what that would be. But he'd find a way, he promised himself.

It was late afternoon before the small group arrived in Dragonwind. Ty took the family to the edge of the woods where Jeb had his cabin and introduced Wilson to Jeb. Jeb was happy to help the family set up one of his tents for the night, and Ty promised to check on them all tomorrow. He thanked Jeb and headed home.

CHAPTER 8

MINE COLLAPSE

The next morning, Ty met with Jeb, Kyle, and Wilson. Addressing Wilson, he said, "We need to get your wagon out of the woods and bring it here."

"How big a wagon is it?" asked Jeb.

Wilson said, "It's not very big. It's a special design I came up with. It has a sturdy wheelbase with four wheels, but instead of being pulled by horses or oxen, it's designed to be pulled by one man. It's well balanced and not very heavy. I don't own any horses, and I wanted to be able to move our things by myself."

Jeb thought for a few minutes and then pointed at a large wagon next to his barn. "Any chance it would fit on that wagon?"

Wilson walked over to the wagon and then returned. "Yes, it should. It will hang over a bit, but with some rope, we ought to be able to secure it well enough."

Jeb looked at Kyle, who nodded, and then Jeb said, "How would it be if Kyle and I took you in that wagon and we went to get your things?"

"You'd do that?" asked Wilson, a note of disbelief in his voice.

"Sure," said Jeb. "Why not? I'd love to see your wagon design. I can think of a lot of uses for it."

As the three men got ready to return to the spot where Ty and Wilson had hidden the wagon, Ty said, "I'm going to ride partway with you and then go on to the mining villages. I'm concerned about what I saw and heard yesterday. Something's not right."

"Just be careful," said Wilson. "We left in the dead of night. The mine manager, Johnston, doesn't want anyone to quit working. He's under a lot of pressure from Lord Upworth, and now he's getting really nasty, threatening people if they try to leave. We were lucky to get out."

"Trust me," said Ty, "I can handle myself. I need evidence to take to King Bertram."

Once Jeb had hitched two large draft horses to the wagon, they set off. Ty rode White Star while Jeb, Kyle, and Wilson rode in the wagon. It took them a bit over an hour to find the spot where Wilson's wagon was hidden. It didn't take long for Jeb, Kyle, Ty, and Wilson to lift the wagon up onto Jeb's wagon and secure it.

"See you back in Dragonwind," said Ty as the loaded wagon with Jeb driving headed back down the road.

Ty continued toward the mining villages. He noticed a small campfire off the road under some trees. Curious, he headed toward it. He found a group of families huddled for warmth around the fire. They looked up as he approached, their faces etched with fear.

Ty smiled. "Good morning. How are you?"

One man stepped forward. "We aren't doing anything wrong. Just leave us be."

Ty said, "I just thought maybe I could help. You have some pretty young children here, and it's a long walk to get to any other villages. Do you need help?"

"We're just fine," said the man, and he started to turn away. Just then one of the children started coughing.

"Looks to me as if you could use some help," said Ty. "Are you from the mining villages?"

"What if we were?" said the man who was obviously their spokesperson. "We aren't going back there, and you can't make us."

"I have no intention of making you do anything," said Ty. "I only want to help. I'm from Dragonwind, which is the closest village on this road. I wanted you to know that we'd be happy to help you if we can."

"Why would you do that?" said the man, his voice filled with suspicion.

"Because I'm an ambassador for King Bertram, and we've been hearing some very disturbing rumors about what's going on in those villages. We'd like to be sure that everyone is safe and that no children are put to work down in the mines."

At this point, one of the women, the mother of the coughing child, said, "How far is it to Dragonwind?"

"It's about an hour on horseback, but walking, with children, I'd guess it might take you until late afternoon. I wish I had better transport for you, but I need to move on to your former villages to try to find out what's going on."

"We'll manage," said the man. Then, realizing that he sounded rather churlish, he said, "And thanks for telling us about Dragonwind."

"I'll be coming back this way once I've seen what's going on in the villages, so maybe then I could get you more help," said Ty.

Ty headed up the road as the small group began packing up and putting out their campfire. He hoped they'd be all right, but he really did have to try to find Johnston and discover the truth of the situation at the mines.

It took him another hour to reach the area where the four villages, more like hamlets really, were located. The place looked deserted. Then Ty heard a loud roar followed by thunderous crashing sounds that seemed to be coming from a nearby mine shaft.

Ty watched as the shaft started to collapse. He could hear cries for help and raced over to assist however he could. Several men ran out of the mine, and Ty shouted, "What happened?"

The men looked startled, and then one of them said, "Nothing. It's just another collapse."

"Is anyone still inside?" asked Ty.

"No," said the man, "and it's none of your business."

"I'm able to help," said Ty, "if someone needs rescuing."

"Just get out of here. I have things under control," snarled the man.

"Are you Johnston?" asked Ty.

The man looked startled. "What if I am? I'm in charge here."

"So I understand," said Ty. "I've been sent by King Bertram. We understand that there have been some problems here, and we want to see if we can help."

"This is private property, and you have no rights here. Lord Upworth won't be happy with any interference."

Then there was another loud roar, which Ty recognized as coming from a moose. He sent out a telepathic query as he noticed the scared looks on two of the men's faces. *Who's there? Do you need help?*

Yes, please. Now. There are children trapped in the mine.

Ty looked at Johnston. "There are children trapped in there."

"So what?" said Johnston. "They'll be dead soon. It's their own fault. They probably brought the mine down on themselves by bumping a support."

"What?" shouted Ty. "How can you be so unfeeling?"

Then Ty said, *How can I help? Where are you?*

I'm at the rear entrance to the mine. Hurry.

Ty took off around the mine, and soon he saw a very large moose pawing at the ground. Ty could see where the entrance had collapsed, and he rushed forward. *How many are in there?* he asked.

There are six of them, and they're not far in, said the moose. *I'd warned them to run when I felt the ground shifting. I can speak like this with one of the boys.*

Ty looked around and saw a shed that held tools. He grabbed a pick and a shovel and returned to the moose. *Where should I dig?*

The moose pawed the ground in front of her, and Ty dug as quickly as he could. He wished he had help, but Johnston and his crew weren't going to do a thing. However, as he started to dig, several women ran over.

"Can you help?" shouted Ty. "Grab some shovels and help me dig."

Soon there were six of them, digging as fast as they could. Ty followed directions from the moose who was in contact with one of the trapped boys, and he was so happy to have her information.

Paul says there's an air pocket where they're trapped but that the air is starting to feel very stale, the moose reported.

Ty and the women dug faster. As they worked, Ty said, *I'm Ty, from Dragonwind. I'm sure glad you're here.*

The moose nodded. *I'm glad you're here too. I'm Wilhelmina, and this isn't the first mine collapse to occur here. This is just the first one where we might stand a chance of saving them, so I'm glad you're here also.*

They'd been digging for nearly an hour when Wilhelmina said, *Stop. You're really close. Use your hands now.*

Ty relayed this information to the women, and they dug more carefully by hand. Soon they found one arm sticking up through the dirt, and they saw movement indicating more digging from underneath. They worked quickly, and soon they were pulling out the first child. After that, they were able to open up a hole, and they saw the other five children. Ty jumped down into the hole and carefully lifted up each child. He was not at all surprised to discover that the women who'd been digging so hard were the mothers of these children.

That's all of them, said Wilhelmina.

Ty got out of the hole and then went to each child. He was horrified to discover just how young they were. There were four boys and two girls, and Ty thought that they all were under eight years old. He checked them for injuries. One of the girls had a broken arm, and two of the boys had broken legs. Everyone had many scrapes and cuts.

"Is there anywhere we can take them to get them cleaned and treated?" asked Ty. "Do you have a healer here?"

One of the women said, "We used to until Lord Upworth said that she wasn't welcome anymore. She'd tried to get safer working conditions for the children."

Another woman said, "My home is the largest. It's not much, but we can take them there."

Ty started to pick up one of the boys with a broken leg, when Wilhelmina said, *You may put the children on my back, and I'll carry them to the woman's house.*

Ty seemed surprised but readily agreed. He carefully placed the two boys with broken legs and the one girl with a broken arm on Wilhelmina's back. The mothers weren't sure about the plan, but the children said they knew Wilhelmina. Ty then carried a fourth child, who had a nasty cut on his head. The mothers carried the other two, and soon they were at the home of the mother who'd volunteered shelter.

Ty carried the children one at a time from Wilhelmina's back, and he noticed that one of the boys with a broken leg said, *Thanks, Wilhelmina. You saved us!*

Once everyone was inside, the boy who'd spoken to Wilhelmina said, "Leave the door open so Wilhelmina can watch."

Ty nodded. The mothers were bustling around setting up makeshift beds on the floor of the main room. Ty then went from one injured child to the next. He healed minor cuts and abrasions and then set to work on the broken bones. Two of the breaks, the arm and one of the legs, were clean breaks, and once Ty found splints, he had them set, and the children were much more comfortable.

However, the other leg break, Paul's, the boy with telepathic abilities, was much worse, with the bone sticking out of his skin. Ty looked at the young man. "How old are you?"

"I'll be seven this winter," answered Paul.

"Well, you're old enough to know that this is going to hurt," said Ty gently. "I can help you, but first we need to convince this bone to go back where it belongs. I'll be as gentle as I can be, but maybe it would help you to talk and pretend I'm not here. Why don't you tell me what happened in the mine."

Paul nodded. "OK."

As Ty readied the splints and found the other supplies he needed, Paul began. "You know I can talk with Wilhelmina, right?"

"Yes," said Ty. "What you can do is called telepathy."

Paul said, "Just before the collapse, Wilhelmina called to me that something was going to fall, that the ground was shaking. I told the others to head for the back exit. We knew we couldn't get to the front. I saw one of the support poles starting to tip, so I grabbed it, trying to hold it up until the others were past me. Once they'd gotten past, well, I couldn't hold it anymore and so I ran as I let go. I was nearly past the pole when it fell on me. I think that's when my leg broke. Roy, the redhead over there, grabbed my arms and pulled me free. We were trapped in a small cavern. That's when I heard Wilhelmina's first roar."

Ty had been working quickly but carefully, as he had to cut Paul's leg to make room to put the bone back. Mercifully, Paul slipped into unconsciousness as he began the incision. When Ty was ready, he asked Paul's mother to grab his ankle and pull as Ty pulled on Paul's upper leg. It took a lot of strength, but finally, the bone snapped back into place. Ty worked fast then to stitch the wound and splint the leg. He was just finishing when Paul woke up.

"You were really brave, Paul," said Ty, "and you're a hero who saved lives today. You should be very proud of that."

Paul gave a weak smile, and his mother hugged him.

Ty stepped out of the room to talk with Wilhelmina. *I need to get back to Dragonwind today and then contact King Bertram. I'm horrified about what's going on here. How strong are your telepathic powers? Can you reach me in Dragonwind?*

Wilhelmina seemed to smile before she said, *You mean where you, Rupert, Samantha, Foxy, Criseda, and others, including Esme, live. For sure. I've never bothered you—moose prefer to live alone—but I know all about you, and yes, you're safe to go to Dragonwind and start cleaning up this mess. I'll let you know if there are any problems here, either with that jerk Johnston or with any of the injured children.*

Ty was amazed by Wilhelmina's answer. *Thank you, and thank you for looking after these children. I'm going to tell Johnston that the mine is to stay closed for now, until it can be inspected.*

He won't like that, but tonight, I'll go stomping around and there will be enough damage that he won't be able to open it.

Ty nodded, but then felt he should add, *Please be careful. We need you. These men are truly nasty, and you may be big, but an arrow or two would be disastrous for you.*

You take care as well. I think you're a bigger threat to them than I am.

See you soon, said Ty.

Ty talked with Paul and his mother. "I have to leave to get help, but Wilhelmina can reach me in Dragonwind, so if you need anything, for the injured children or to deal with Johnston, just let Wilhelmina know, and I'll be back."

Paul's mother, a young woman named Naomi, said, "I never really believed that Paul could talk to Wilhelmina. I thought it was just make believe. But I'm so grateful to her and to you."

"I'll be back," said Ty, "and things will be changed around here. Just take care of Paul. That was a nasty break, and I don't want the wound to get infected. Please let me know if there's any change in his condition or if he starts to run a fever. If that happens, I'll get both him and you to Dragonwind so that my friend Martha can help him."

Once he'd received assurances from all the mothers that they would let Wilhelmina know if anyone was not healing well, Ty and White Star went back to the front of the mine. Johnston and the others were still there, and Ty said, "No thanks to you, we rescued all six children. The mine is now closed until it can be inspected. I'm going to confer with King Bertram, and then I'll be back."

"You can't tell us what to do," said Johnston. "We don't take our orders from you."

"I have the king's authority, and that trumps your boss. Don't do any mining until things have been inspected."

With that, Ty and White Star rode away toward Dragonwind.

CHAPTER 9

REFUGEES

Ty and White Star were nearing home when they came upon the group of refugees they'd seen in the morning. The families looked very tired. Ty stopped and talked to their leader.

"You're nearly to Dragonwind. Sorry I wasn't here sooner, but I had to help rescue six young children from a mine collapse," Ty said.

"Yet another one," said the man. "I'm glad you were there. Johnston doesn't allow any rescue attempts."

"So I gathered," said Ty. "I'm sorry. In any case, I'm going to ride ahead and get some folks to come out with wagons to help you the last bit of the way, and we'll get you settled. I'll be right back."

"Thank you," said the man.

Ty rode on quickly and arrived at Jeb's. He asked Jeb and Kyle if they would help bring the families into Dragonwind, and they readily agreed. Wilson said he'd bring his wagon as well. He'd spent the afternoon repairing its broken axle.

The four of them, with two large wagons and Wilson's smaller one, caught up to the travelers about two miles outside of Dragonwind. The families were happy to see a familiar face, and Wilson assured them that the folks in Dragonwind were kind and helpful.

Soon the group of wagons entered Dragonwind and stopped in the center of the village, in front of the village green. Several people came out to see what was going on, and Ty said, "These people need our help. They're fleeing from a bad situation in the mining villages. If you have anywhere they could shelter, a spare room in your home or even space in your barns, we'll get them settled for the night. They're very tired and hungry, and at least one of the children needs to see Martha for his cough."

Ty was pleased to see that his fellow villagers immediately sprang into action. Martha and Kyle took charge of organizing things, counting heads, making lists of available lodging, requesting donations of food and blankets, and many other details. It was decided that a meal would be served in the village hall, as the central location would make it easier to feed everyone.

The travelers were brought to the hall as the villagers began preparations. Martha went to the hall to check on the health of the travelers, and she found several small children with nasty coughs.

One of the mothers said, "They were forced to work in the mines. But finally, this morning, we decided no more, and we left our homes before daylight."

Martha examined the children. "I have a cough syrup that should soothe them. They aren't sick, thankfully, but it will take a few days, maybe even a few weeks, for them to clear out the mine dust from their lungs. The coughing is actually helpful in expelling the debris, but now their throats are raw from the coughing. My syrup will help with that irritation."

Martha opened her bag with her medicines and began dosing the children. Then she asked if anyone else needed help. No one did, so Martha left to check on the arrangements.

Ty was still out on the village green when several villagers came up to him. One of the men said, "How are we supposed to help all these people? It's nearly winter, and we have only enough to get our own families through the season. There's no room for more people."

Ty looked at the small group and took a deep breath. He was glad that most of the villagers felt that helping was the right thing to do, but Ty supposed there would always be those who could see only their own needs. He said, "I've been to their homes. They've been living under brutal conditions. If the situations were reversed, I'm sure they'd help you."

"Maybe," said Drake, who seemed to be the spokesman for this group, "but the situations aren't reversed. We've worked hard for what we have, and we're not sharing. Just wanted you to know that. You can't make us."

"No, Drake," said Ty, sadness evident in his voice. "I have no intention of making anyone do anything. However, when your neighbors are all pitching in to make a difference for these folks and you selfishly refuse, you may find that your neighbors feel differently about you. It's your choice. Now if you'll excuse me, I need to help Martha and Kyle organize things."

With that, Ty turned his back on the men and walked away.

When Ty reached Martha and Kyle, he found that everything was well organized. The travelers had each been assigned sleeping accommodations and now they were in the village hall. Washing facilities had been set up for them, and tables were being laid with dishes and food.

Ty noticed that the travelers were looking rather stunned by the outpouring of help and kindness that they were receiving. He suspected that they'd lived under Johnston's rule for so long that they'd forgotten what most people were capable of. Of course, there were always the Drakes around, but Ty was glad to see that most of the villagers were not like him.

Ty went to find Miranda to see if she could send a message to King Bertram via the fox communication network. She was happy to do so and listened as Ty updated her on what had happened at the mine collapse and what actions he'd taken.

I've got it, said Miranda. *For the sake of accuracy, I'm going to send several shorter messages, as there's a lot of information to convey. I take it the most important thing is to alert King Bertram to your closing of the mines so that he can inform Lord Upworth?*

Yes, said Ty. *I'm a bit concerned about what Johnston might do now. I would go to the palace, but I really feel that I need to be back in the mining hamlets tomorrow morning to check on the children and see what's going on.*

May I suggest you take Criseda? asked Miranda. *She'll make an impression, and she's also a lot faster than White Star.*

I agree, said Ty, and he left her to send the messages to King Bertram.

The evening went smoothly, and the travelers were all settled, so grateful for the food and the chance to sleep. Ty went to his cave, fed Foxy, and headed for bed. He was wakened several hours before dawn by a telepathic call from Wilhelmina.

Ty, you need to get here quickly.

What's happened? said Ty a bit groggily as he struggled to come fully awake.

Last night a rider arrived from Lord Upworth, said Wilhelmina. *He spoke to Johnston. Then Johnston and his men burned down most of the buildings in the hamlets, including the general store. We've been fighting the blazes and just now have them under control, but people are homeless, including the children you rescued. Also, Johnston and his men have left. I don't know where they went, but they left with Lord Upworth's messenger. We need help, and we need it fast. It's cold.*

On my way, said Ty. *Criseda and I will be with you in about half an hour. Are there any wagons or horses left in the mining towns?*

No, they were taken away weeks ago, answered Wilhelmina. *The few that were still here have been burned.*

OK, let the villagers know that help is coming.

Thanks, Ty.

Ty dressed quickly and headed to Jeb's. As he went, he called to Criseda. *We need to fly to the mining towns now. I'll let you know what's been going on as we travel, but we have villagers who are now homeless and need help.*

Be right there, answered Criseda without hesitation.

Ty woke Jeb and explained what had happened. He asked Jeb to see if he could round up villagers who might be willing to drive wagons to the mining towns to rescue the remaining people.

"Certainly," said Jeb. "Do you have any idea how many people we're talking about?"

Ty said, "Let me ask Wilhelmina." *Wilhelmina, how many people do you have there?*

There are only three men, and they are quite old, said Wilhelmina. *There are thirteen women, all widows of miners killed in the mines. Eight of the women have children, including the six you rescued. There are another five children, three of whom are infants. So the grand total is three men, thirteen women, and eleven children, for a total of twenty-seven villagers.*

Got it, thanks, answered Ty, and he turned to Jeb to relay the information to him. "Bottom line," he concluded, "we need transport for sixteen adults and eleven children, all under the age of about eight."

"OK," said Jeb. "I'm on it." He headed out of his cabin to begin waking those with horses and wagons who he thought would help.

Ty went to Martha's and woke her. "I've got to go get the rest of the people from the mining towns. They've become homeless after Johnston and his men burned the towns. Jeb is organizing transport." Ty gave her the numbers on those needing help. "If you can be ready for them when they arrive, that would be most helpful. I suspect they won't be here until after dark, as it will take Jeb and his wagons all morning to get there, and then the return trip will take at least as long."

"Don't worry, Ty," said Martha. "We'll be ready for them, and I'll also get some blankets and food to send with Jeb and his crew. Those poor people."

"I know," said Ty. "Criseda and I are on our way now. See you later."

He gave her a quick hug and headed out to the village green, where Criseda was waiting for him.

As they flew, Ty told her all that had happened over the last few days. When he finished, Criseda said, *I know people can be selfish and cruel, but there's something deeply wrong here. The number of mine collapses is excessive by anyone's standards. And the refusal to rescue anyone caught in a collapse also seems bizarre. After all, if Lord Upworth needs the mines for income, and he needs slave labor to work the mines, why would he be killing off his labor and wrecking his mines?*

Good question, said Ty. *I've been so busy just going from one disaster to the next that I hadn't stopped to analyze it.*

There used to be a lot more people living in those mining towns. I mean, they weren't as big as Dragonwind, even with all four combined, but people have been leaving there in droves, and now there are just twenty-seven remaining. This isn't right.

We have more questions than answers, agreed Ty. *Let's get these folks back to Dragonwind, and then you and I can search for the truth about what's going on.*

They landed near the previous day's mine collapse, and Ty was horrified to see the total destruction of all the buildings. There hadn't been many, but they were now all burned to the ground. The remaining villagers were clustered around a campfire, trying to stay warm. It wasn't yet dawn, and the autumn night had been cold, with the season's first freeze.

Ty saw Naomi and went over to talk to her. "Was anyone hurt?"

Naomi shook her head. "No, thanks again to Wilhelmina and my son. Wilhelmina was keeping an eye on Johnston, as I suspect you knew. When a messenger arrived from Lord Upworth, Wilhelmina overheard the man giving orders that Johnston was to burn everything to the ground. Wilhelmina kept roaring until she'd wakened us all. She told Paul what was happening, and he told us. We managed to get everyone outside just ahead of the flames, but all we own is now gone."

"I'm so sorry, but I'm very glad it's not any worse," said Ty. Then he turned to Wilhelmina, who was standing protectively next to where Paul was lying. "Thank you, Wilhelmina, and thank you, Paul."

"What do we do now?" said Paul, and Ty could tell he was shivering in the cold.

Ty spoke to the entire group. "There are wagons coming from Dragonwind to take you out of here. Wilhelmina alerted us so we'd know your plight, and we're going to take care of you. That's the good news.

"The hard part is that the wagons will take several hours to get here. I don't think, realistically, that we can expect them before noon. They will have food and blankets, but that's still a long time, especially for those who are injured." As he said this, he looked down at Paul.

Ty continued. "What I'd like to do is have my dragon, Criseda, start taking those who are suffering the most back to Dragonwind."

Many of the villagers looked alarmed at the suggestion, but Ty said, "She'll transport you quickly and gently, and my friends in Dragonwind will be able to help on the other end."

Ty began walking among the villagers, assessing their health. He was worried about Paul as well as the older men, who must have been miners when they were younger and who all had wheezing coughs and were shivering.

Finally, he said, "I think Paul and one of you men should go first, if you're willing."

Paul immediately nodded yes, but it took a while to find one of the men who would agree. Once the two were chosen, Ty helped the old man up first and then lifted Paul as gently as he could, being careful of his leg. Ty asked the man, whose name was Tim, to hold on to Paul. Once they were situated, Criseda slowly took off, and everyone watched in amazement as the pair disappeared.

Ty built up the fire with whatever wood he could find before talking to the other two men. "I'd like you to be next. Are you willing?"

They looked at each other, and finally one of them said, "We can't let Tim have all the bragging rights."

Ty went over to Naomi and said, "Criseda could also take one of your infants if you thought that either of those men would carry her."

Naomi said, "Little Angelica is Rob's granddaughter, so he'd certainly take her."

Ty nodded, and when Criseda returned about an hour later, the two men and Angelica were put on her back, and again she left.

Criseda needed an hour to make a round trip, but the wagons would take a good five hours, so she was able to make several more trips before the first of the wagons arrived. Ty had sent all the children on Criseda, as they were the ones most in need of food and warmth. In addition, the ones who'd been caught in the mine collapse were showing signs of distress after all they'd been through, even the three who had suffered only minor scrapes and cuts.

Jeb, Wilson, and Kyle distributed the blankets and food they'd brought and then settled the remaining villagers into the three wagons. Thanks to Criseda's efforts, there was plenty of room for the women to stretch out, and some of them even tried to sleep on the way to Dragonwind. It had been a very long night for them.

Wilhelmina walked beside the wagons, and she told Ty, *Paul is excited about his ride on Criseda. Thank you. I'm concerned that he's developed a fever, but I hope you and Martha will heal him. See you in Dragonwind. I hope there's room for a big moose.*

Ty laughed and rubbed her forehead. *Of course there is!*

CHAPTER 10

THREATS

Ty and Criseda returned to Dragonwind and let Sara know that the last of the refugees were on their way and should be arriving by nightfall. Sara thanked him. "Martha is taking care of the sick. She asked me to send you to her as soon as you arrived. She's worried about Paul."

Ty thanked her and headed to Martha's. He entered through the kitchen door and then headed to the guest bedroom where he could hear both Martha's and Esme's voices. As he entered the room, Esme jumped up and ran to hug him. "Paul's really, really sick. Can you heal him?"

Ty looked toward the bed and couldn't help but compare the situation to their previous worry over Esme. Again they had a young child with a broken leg and a raging fever.

Martha looked up from applying a fresh poultice to Paul's leg. She looked exhausted and very worried. "I'm really glad you're here. He's not responding to my treatments. He's having nightmares as well and wakes up shouting, 'I won't tell. I promise. Don't hurt my mom.' We have no idea who he's talking to or what it's all about. Can you talk telepathically to him?"

Ty tried but then shook his head. "I can't reach him."

"Neither can I," said Esme, "and neither can Rupert or Samantha."

Ty considered the situation and then spoke to Wilhelmina. *Can you shed any light on this? Do you know what Paul's so afraid of?*

It didn't take long before Wilhelmina answered. *Unfortunately, yes, I do, and I blame myself. He should never have had to shoulder the burden he's bearing. He and I discovered, quite by accident, that Lord Upworth had instructed Johnston to place wooden chests inside most of the mine shafts and then to knock the shafts down. The only way to get the chests into the shafts was to have children take them in. The passages were too narrow for an adult.*

Lord Upworth also didn't trust the adults. So we watched as Paul's friends were used to move the chests into the mines. Three or four children would take a chest in, pushing and shoving it, until it was placed to Johnston's satisfaction. Then Johnston instructed the children to bury the chest, and while they were doing that, he would knock down the supports and bury the children. Lord Upworth wanted no witnesses.

Ty said, *That's horrible. How long has that been going on?*

Wilhelmina said, *Paul and I just discovered it after the last mine collapse before yesterday's. We heard Johnston instructing four of Paul's friends and threatening them with harm to their families if they ever said what they'd done. We hadn't realized until it was too late that Johnston would kill the children. After that collapse, Paul and I dug for the chest, late at night after everyone was asleep. We found a chest filled with money. I assume all the others contain the same as well. We removed the one we'd uncovered, and I hid it where it won't be found.*

Ty thought for a moment. *So yesterday, when Paul and the other five went into the mine, Paul knew he'd be killed.*

Yes, said Wilhelmina, *he did, and still he went. He kept in constant contact with me, and he was determined he'd find a way out. He was determined to save his friends, and thanks to you, he did. But now he's reliving the entire nightmare, not only of his own nearly fatal trip into the mines but also all the others where children were killed.*

Can you talk to him? Ty asked. *Can you reassure him at all? Nothing we're doing seems to be helping him.*

I'll try, answered Wilhelmina, who then directed her telepathy just to Paul.

While Wilhelmina was trying to reach Paul, Ty told Martha and Esme what he'd learned. Martha couldn't believe anyone would have done such a thing, but Esme started shaking. "The Wraith would, or he'd make others do it."

Martha left to get a fresh poultice, and Ty and Esme waited, Esme using a cool cloth on Paul's head. Then she said, "I asked Paul if we could talk telepathically. I thought it would be cool to have a friend with magic. But he couldn't. I guess the only one he can talk with is Wilhelmina."

Ty could hear the disappointment in her voice, and he understood it. His only telepathic friends had been woodland creatures. He'd continued to hope for the longest time that Jeb would learn how to talk telepathically, but that never happened.

Wilhelmina contacted Ty. *I'm trying. Paul's slipping away from me as well, but I'm holding fast to him. I'm reassuring him that he's safe now and that no one can harm him or his mother. His mother is really worried. This wagon ride isn't helping her.*

Ty turned to Martha. "Paul needs his mother. If he's worried that she's in danger, he might be comforted by her presence."

"Makes sense," said Martha. "When will she arrive?"

"Not until evening," said Ty, "Although given how sick Paul is, maybe Criseda and I should fly out to the wagons and bring her back sooner."

Martha nodded. "Frankly, he might not last until evening unless Wilhelmina can hang on to him."

Ty headed out of the cottage and called to Criseda. *We need to bring Paul's mother back here as quickly as we can.*

Criseda landed, and Ty vaulted onto her back. They took off, and Criseda flew as quickly as she could while Ty told Wilhelmina, *We're on our way to you. We'll take Paul's mother directly to him.*

That's good. I'm not sure how much longer I can hold him. But I'll let him know that his mother is safe and is coming to him. Good luck!

About fifteen minutes later, the caravan of wagons came into view. Wilhelmina saw Ty and Criseda and said, *Naomi's in the middle wagon.*

Thanks, said Ty as they landed. He went over to the middle wagon. "Naomi, Paul needs you. We can fly you to him if you're willing."

Naomi looked apprehensively at Criseda but then she took a deep breath before she nodded. "If Paul can ride a dragon, then so can I. Just tell me what to do."

Ty helped her onto Criseda's back and then vaulted up behind her. "Don't worry. Criseda won't let you fall and neither will I, but she's going to fly as fast as she can. Paul's really sick, and he needs you."

Naomi took a deep breath and nodded. Criseda did fly really fast, and they were even aided by a tailwind, so it wasn't long before they were landing in Dragonwind.

Thanks, Criseda, said Ty as he jumped down and helped Naomi off Criseda's back. Naomi looked at Criseda. "Thank you for taking both Paul and me."

Criseda dipped her head in a bow. Ty hurried Naomi over to Martha's cottage, taking her into the kitchen and then through to the guest bedroom. Naomi quietly entered the room, followed by Ty. Esme stood and offered her chair to Naomi, who sat by Paul's head and held his hand.

Martha, who was just finishing changing yet another poultice, said, "Talk to him. Maybe sing to him. He's worried about your safety, and he's scared."

Esme handed Naomi a fresh, cool cloth, and then Esme, Ty, and Martha stepped out of the room. They went into the kitchen, and Martha said, "So what now?"

"I need to get back up to the mines to see if I can find more chests. We'll need to take them so that we have some leverage over Lord Upworth," said Ty. "But I don't want to leave while Paul is in danger. I don't know how much help my healing magic will be, but obviously his fever needs to break."

"I should go check in with Sara," said Martha. "She took over for me when Paul became so ill."

Ty looked at her and then pulled out a chair from the kitchen table. "You need to rest for a few minutes. You're exhausted. Sara was fine when I last saw her. The wagons won't be here for several more hours. I'll make you some tea. Have you eaten recently?"

Martha seemed to sag into the chair. "I don't know. All I can think about is that poor boy. What he's been through—no one should have had to go through that and certainly not a seven-year-old."

Then Martha looked over at Esme. "You're another one who's had a lifetime of sorrow already. I can't believe what the two of you have experienced. And all those children killed. It's too much to take in."

Ty brought tea to Martha and then set about making sandwiches for them all. "You're right about that," he said. "But we'll get to the bottom of it all. And Esme, Paul, and all the others will have safe, happy lives from now on if King Bertram and I have anything to say about it."

Wilhelmina interrupted the discussion. *Thank you for bringing Naomi. Paul's responding a bit now. She's singing lullabies to him and bathing his forehead, and he seems to be coming into a better place. Martha will be able to tell for sure, but I think his fever is coming down.*

Ty relayed this information to Martha, who immediately stood up and went to Paul's room. Esme and Ty followed her. Everyone was relieved to see that Paul's eyes were open and he was staring at his mother. Martha checked his fever and confirmed that it was dissipating.

Ty was relieved. He told Wilhelmina, *You were right. His fever is coming down. I think he's safe now. Do you know where the other chests are buried? If Criseda and I go back to the mines, could you guide us telepathically to them? We need to take them before Lord Upworth decides that maybe they aren't safe where they are.*

I believe I can guide you, said Wilhelmina. *I can send you telepathic maps to the locations, and I don't think it will be hard for you to find the collapsed sinkholes that used to be mine entrances. I can also guide you to the hiding spot for the one Paul and I took. Then you can decide what to do with them.*

Ty looked at Martha and motioned for her to come out into the hallway. Once they were out of earshot of Paul and Naomi, Ty said quietly, "Criseda and I are going back to the mines to find the other chests. Wilhelmina says she can guide us telepathically. She can also call us if you need us, so don't hesitate to give a shout if anything changes here. Meanwhile," he finished with a smile creeping across his face, "you might want to figure out how you're going to get Paul and Wilhelmina together. Maybe she can put her head through a window, but I guarantee those two will not be kept apart any more than Esme can be kept from Rupert and Samantha."

Martha groaned and then smiled. "I might just as well move us all to a barn! Good luck with the chests."

CHAPTER 11

TREASURE

It didn't take long for Ty and Criseda to return to the mines. They had several hours of daylight left, so they set to work immediately. Ty had brought picks and shovels because he wasn't sure any of the tools that had been in the mines' toolshed would have survived the fire.

We're here, Wilhelmina, said Ty.

OK, she answered, *I've been thinking over the past several weeks. There have been six cave-ins, so I'm guessing that means that there are five more chests, since Paul and I already got one. Here's the map I've made in my mind.*

Ty focused as Wilhelmina sent him a picture of the villages with the spots of the various mine collapses clearly shown. Ty concentrated on the image she sent and then looked at the actual physical scene. He turned himself so that he was oriented in the same direction as her image. He could see clearly several of the spots on her map.

Thanks, Wilhelmina. We'll start digging now and keep you posted. I think I've found three of the spots already.

With that, Criseda and Ty began working. Although Ty had a shovel, he soon discovered that the claws on Criseda's front legs were much more effective, now that they didn't have to worry about collapsing more tunnels or saving children.

They worked quickly, but it was sad work. The first spot yielded not only a chest but also four bodies.

Wilhelmina, we can bury the children's bodies, but is that what the parents would want? Do you have any idea? asked Ty.

Could you put them all together and then bury them enough so that predators can't get to them? Then when you get back, we could try to locate their parents and ask them, said Wilhelmina. *Some of the first children to be taken into the mines were orphans. Others had parents, but those parents were among the first to leave the villages, and I have no idea where they are now.*

I understand, said Ty. *We'll figure out something that's both respectful and allows us to return for them if that's needed. Thanks.*

Criseda dug a long trench six feet deep, and as they uncovered bodies, Ty carefully placed them in the trench. As he did so, he sent mental images of each child to Wilhelmina, who in turn gave him the child's name. Ty carefully logged each one in his notebook, with a drawing showing the body's placement in the trench.

It took them about three hours to find all five chests, and it was heartbreaking to lay twenty-three children in the trench. Criseda carefully covered the bodies so that no predators could reach them, and Ty placed stones on the mound to mark the location.

Once this was done, Ty called to Wilhelmina. *Where did you put the last chest?*

Again, Wilhelmina sent him a map, and he went off to find it while Criseda stood guard over the five they'd uncovered. Ty didn't have any difficulty locating the last chest, and he decided that he and Criseda needed to take the chests back to Dragonwind.

Criseda said, *I think I should take these to the dragons. They will keep them safe from anyone, even The Wraith, until you and King Bertram decide what's to happen with them.*

That's an excellent idea, agreed Ty.

Ty began tying the chests to Criseda. It was a difficult task. Some he tied to her back, but three of them had to be slung under her belly. Thankfully, the chests weren't outrageously heavy, as they were meant to be moved by small children. Nevertheless, six of them weighed as much as three men. And Ty would add to that weight, as he'd need to ride as well.

Are you sure you can take all this at once? Ty asked apprehensively.

We'll see, won't we? she replied, and Ty could hear the hesitation in her voice.

Let's see how well it goes. We can always stop once we're away from this spot, if you need to, said Ty as he carefully climbed onto her back.

Criseda's takeoff was the hardest part, but after a wobbly start, she gained altitude and then took advantage of the tailwind, gliding whenever she could to conserve strength. She cut a direct path to the dragons' home, which was closer to the mines than Dragonwind. Ty leaned along her neck to cut down on as much wind resistance as he could. The journey was slower than he would have liked, and he was worried about Criseda's endurance. She was a younger dragon, and this was asking a lot of her.

They'd been flying for over an hour when Ty spotted the crags of the dragons' home. He was so relieved to see other dragons there. Foster, a young green dragon, flew over to them, and Ty quickly told him what they were doing. Criseda needed all her strength just to stay in the air.

Foster took off back to the dragons' home, and soon Magnolia, a very large and beautiful yellow dragon, arrived. She said, *Criseda, you're nearly home. I'm going to fly below you, and if needed I can take all your weight and bring you in safely, but I'll give you the opportunity to do it on your own. We're really proud of you, and now you're safe.*

That reassurance seemed to be all Criseda needed. True to her word, Magnolia stayed right below Criseda as the two of them glided to the landing area in the dragons' aerie. Magnolia pulled back and up so that Criseda could land, and although the landing was a bit bumpy, no one commented on it.

Ty immediately jumped down and began untying the chests. Criseda was too exhausted to explain anything, but thankfully, Magnolia seemed to know what was needed. Sapphire, a lovely large bluish-purple dragon, came over and greeted Ty.

Well, youngling, what can we do for you? she asked.

Ty quickly explained about the chests and the need to hide them. Sapphire agreed but added, *You'll stay here tonight, and then tomorrow we need to talk.*

Ty agreed. He was extremely grateful to the dragons for all they'd done for him throughout his life, but he also realized that Sapphire wasn't asking him; she was telling him.

Ty contacted Wilhelmina. *We have the six chests, and the dragons are going to keep them until we decide what to do with them. Meanwhile, I'm going to stay with the dragons tonight. Are things OK in Dragonwind?*

Yes, answered Wilhelmina. *Paul is able to eat some broth, and Martha, bless her, has Kyle working on widening the window in his room so that I can get my head inside. Paul wants to sleep with me, but I think for tonight, he should stay in a bed. Maybe tomorrow we'll figure something else out.*

Let Martha, Esme, and Kyle know that Criseda and I are fine and I'll see them tomorrow, said Ty.

The next morning, Ty met with Criseda, Sapphire, and Magnolia. Sapphire, as the leader of the dragons, began by saying, *We need to be sure that the boundaries we set for interactions with humans are clear in the current crisis.*

Ty nodded. *I know, and I'm trying not to ask Criseda for help that puts her in an awkward position. But honestly, if she hadn't helped with the digging and then the burying of the bodies, I wouldn't have been able to accomplish much of anything.*

I understand that, said Sapphire, *but then it wasn't our problem. Neither was moving the injured from the mines to Dragonwind. We aren't here to make your life easier.*

Ty looked down at the ground and mumbled, *I'm sorry. I shouldn't have asked.*

Sapphire chuckled. *You should know that I did give permission for all Criseda's recent activities. I'm just trying to put things in perspective and make sure you don't overstep our boundaries or start taking Criseda's help for granted.*

I promise, said Ty.

Sapphire continued. *We're not at all happy about what's going on in your world. We also want this madman, The Wraith, stopped for the good of the planet. Some of his activities are displacing wildlife. There have been unexplained fires, including the destruction of the mining towns, and those fires have hurt more than humans. In addition, anyone who's willing to use slave labor, especially that of children, and then kill them to keep their secrets is someone who's capable of extreme destruction. He must be stopped.*

Ty said, *Thank you. And thank you for keeping the chests. I was afraid that if it became known that I'd removed them to Dragonwind, it would put a lot of innocents in danger.*

Agreed, said Sapphire.

You should also beware, said Magnolia, *that not all those in Dragonwind are innocents. The influence of The Wraith has spread all through the nation of Estrea.*

Do you know of anyone specifically? asked Ty.

I think you'll be able to figure that out for yourself, possibly with the help of Esme, said Magnolia.

We want Esme protected at all costs, said Sapphire. *Her gift will greatly benefit the planet as a whole, and when she's an adult, she'll make some vital contributions to life in general.*

Ty knew he wouldn't get anymore information than that, so he asked another question. *Do you know anything about Paul? I was surprised to discover that he was telepathic, but his gifts seem to be limited to Wilhelmina. Is that correct?*

Sapphire and Magnolia both chuckled. Sapphire said, *Wilhelmina is a force all her own. She's a strong force for good, and she has amazing powers, similar to what you found with Sterling, the magical stag, but in Wilhelmina's case, she herself is very real, and she will not disappear as Sterling did. She will have an extraordinarily long life. She chooses those she bonds with, and her choice was Paul. It was a very good choice, as he's already a strong and brave young boy with a good heart. But Paul is telepathic only because Wilhelmina has leant him that power.*

Ty nodded. *So Criseda can help me figure out what's going on, especially with The Wraith?*

Yes, said Sapphire. *She's proven herself capable of deciding when her help is appropriate and when it might be too much. Criseda, you will continue to check in with us before taking any actions.*

Criseda nodded.

Sapphire looked carefully at Ty. *When we chose Criseda to be a companion for you, we were, to be honest, looking for a way to forge a closer link between our races. It's obvious that humans have tremendous power for both good and evil and that the use of their powers will affect more than just humans. We are guardians of the planet and all life on it, which does include humans, but for the most part, we've kept to looking after everyone except humans, leaving them to their own devices. We're starting to rethink that strategy now that humans are growing in both number and power.*

Ty was silent for a few minutes. *I think I understand, and I'll never take Criseda for granted. She's such a good friend, and she's always been there for me as I hope I have been for her.*

Understood, said Sapphire. *Now I think you'd better return to Dragonwind, and I think you'll also need to talk with King Bertram. Things are happening that you need to understand.*

With that, Sapphire and Magnolia left the meeting, and Ty vaulted onto Criseda. They flew to Dragonwind to check in.

CHAPTER 12

THE CAPITAL

As soon as Ty and Criseda landed on the village green, Esme, Rupert, and Samantha came running over. Esme gave Ty a big hug. "It's so good to have you back. Come see what's happened."

Esme tugged on Ty's arm, and he laughed and followed her. "How's Paul?"

"You'll see," answered Esme with a smug look as she entered Martha's cottage through the back door.

Ty followed her into the guest room and was pleased to see Paul sitting up in bed with a smile and good color in his face. Then he noticed the open window and saw that Wilhelmina's head completely filled it.

Hi, Wilhelmina, Ty said.

Hi, yourself, she answered back.

Esme, Rupert, and Samantha were seated on Paul's bed, and Naomi was sitting on a chair next to the bed. Martha bustled in with lunch for them all.

As they ate, Ty asked Martha, "What are you going to do at night? This open window will make the room too cold, won't it?"

"Jeb and Kyle are working hard in the barn. They've insulated the walls, taken out the stalls that weren't currently being used, and put in a few room partitions. By evening, Paul, his mother, and Wilhelmina will have accommodations there. It should stay warm and snug for them."

"Wow," said Ty, looking over at Paul. "Sounds as if you're all set."

Paul nodded and ran his hand over Wilhelmina's face. "She's my best friend, and it's so nice of Jeb and Kyle to do this for us. We'll be sharing quarters with Martha's three cows, but we're fine with that. They'll help keep the barn warm."

Ty chuckled. "That they will. I'm sure glad to see you recovering so well."

"Martha says my leg is going to take a while to heal, but Esme, Rupert, and Samantha are keeping Wilhelmina and me company, so we shouldn't be bored. And Wilson says that I can ride in his wagon if I want to get out, which should be fun."

Ty smiled. "Sounds as if you have everything well in hand. I'm really glad."

Ty and Martha left Esme and Paul playing a card game and went to the kitchen.

"I really need to go to the palace and talk with King Bertram," Ty said. "Things look calm here for now, and Wilhelmina can reach me telepathically if needed, so you should be safe."

"I'm sure we'll be fine. The refugees are already settling in well. Some of them want to stay here permanently, if they can find work. Some of them have friends and relations who'd already left and are now in the capital, so they'll probably move on," said Martha.

"I'm sure it will all be sorted out. Magnolia did say that we should watch our backs, that there are folks in Dragonwind who might be working for The Wraith, so be please be very careful."

Martha gave him a hug. "We'll be careful, especially with Esme and Paul, as I realize they're in the greatest danger."

Ty and Criseda flew to the palace, and Ty met with King Bertram to update him.

When the king had heard everything, he said, "I think it's time to talk with Lord Upworth. I've asked Henry to bring him here."

While they waited, Ty asked, "Do you think you can find the parents of any of these children?" He handed over a list of eighteen names. "I found twenty-three bodies, but Wilhelmina let me know that five of them were orphans."

"That's so sad," said King Bertram. "I'll try to discover if their families have come here."

"I made a group burial, but I've kept a drawing of where each one is located. If any of the families want a separate burial, I'll make sure that happens."

"Thanks, Ty."

Henry opened the office door. "Lord Upworth, Your Majesty." He stood aside to let Lord Upworth enter the room.

"You wanted to see me, Bertram?" said Lord Upworth.

"Yes, have a seat."

Once Lord Upworth was seated, King Bertram said, "I've had some very disturbing news about your mines."

"What news? And why is it any of your business?"

"Apparently your mine manager, Johnston, has been using small children in the mines as slave labor. They are forced in there and neither they nor their parents are paid for the work."

"I think you must be mistaken," said Lord Upworth. "My mines have unfortunately stopped producing, and I ordered them closed."

"Are you sure?" said Ty.

Lord Upworth turned to Ty and glared at him. "Of course I am. I'm not used to being disobeyed."

"Do you know that there's been a mass exodus of your villagers? They're fleeing the mining towns," said King Bertram.

"Doesn't surprise me," answered Lord Upworth. "That land isn't good for anything but mining, and now it's not even good for that."

"I was there two days ago when there was another mine collapse," said Ty.

"Couldn't have been," said Lord Upworth. "I ordered the mines closed a month ago."

Ty continued. "Johnston told me not to try to rescue any of the children who were in the mine. He said they were to be left to die under your orders."

"What?" yelled Lord Upworth. "Impossible."

"I dug them out," said Ty. "I rescued six children, thankfully alive, although three of them were badly injured. I was told there'd been five other collapses in the past ten days, all resulting in the deaths of children. Johnston didn't allow any rescue attempts and his men were there to carry out his orders.

"The night after my rescue, a rider came into the village saying he was your messenger. He told Johnston to burn the villages to the ground."

"I sent no messenger," said Lord Upworth, but Ty and the king noticed that he was sounding more unsure and worried.

"Thankfully the few remaining villagers were alerted, and they fled their homes, but they were left to fend for themselves in the cold after Johnston, his men, and your messenger rode off."

Lord Upworth looked confused.

Ty continued. "With the help of some Dragonwind villagers, we managed to rescue the last of your villagers, twenty-seven of them, some severely injured. Then I went back to the mines and found the other five collapses, and I dug. In each of the five, I found the bodies of children, twenty-three of them in all. I also found six chests of money, gold and silver, one in each of the six collapsed mines. One of the children I rescued said that Johnston had made them drag a chest into each mine and then cover it with dirt."

"So, Lord Upworth," said the king, "there's a lot of evidence of horrific criminal activity on your land, led by your mine foreman. What do you have to say?"

"I don't know anything about any of this," Lord Upworth said. "Please, I'm telling the truth. I know you have no reason to believe me. I've fought you on a lot of issues, especially those that I thought were soft on the poor. But murdering children. Forcing them into slave labor. I'd never have allowed that. I thought those mines were closed."

"You didn't make any provisions for the families who were out of work because of your closures, did you?" said Ty.

"Well, no," said Lord Upworth. "That wasn't my job."

"Have you seen Johnston?" said Ty.

"No," said Lord Upworth. "I told him that his services were no longer needed. I didn't expect to see him."

Ty looked at the king and said, telepathically, *Do you believe him?*

I'm not sure, said Bertram. *He did look shocked about the children.*

Ty turned to Lord Upworth. "You do have a reputation for not caring about others, so your callousness doesn't surprise me. But that being said, you still are responsible for what happens on your lands."

"But..." he stammered. "I had no idea. All I did was close the mines."

"Closed the mines and walked away, leaving your miners without any assistance or help, and leaving a mine foreman in charge, someone who has never treated the miners fairly."

"But they were lazy," said Lord Upworth.

"Did you see that for yourself?" asked Ty.

"I read the reports," said Lord Upworth.

"Reports prepared by Johnston?" asked Ty.

"Well, naturally. He was my foreman."

Ty gave Lord Upworth a look of utter contempt.

King Bertram said, "At the very least, you've been criminally negligent. You obviously did not verify anything that you were told. I understand that you're now nearly bankrupt, if rumors are correct. Is that true?"

Lord Upworth looked down at his shoes. "Yes, it is. My investments haven't gone well, and then the mines failed."

"So where did all the money that Ty found in the six chests in your mines come from?" asked Bertram.

"I have no idea," said Lord Upworth. "Believe me, I don't know."

"I suspect Johnston has been robbing you blind for years," said Ty. "And if anyone deserved that, it certainly is you. Unfortunately, twenty-three children paid with their lives to keep that money a secret. And you're responsible for your employees."

Lord Upworth didn't say anything. For once in his life, he seemed to be totally defeated.

Ty looked at King Bertram. *I suspect he's greedy and stupid, but I can't see him doing this.*

I agree, said the king. Then he turned to Lord Upworth. "All your lands are now forfeited to the crown. We will manage them for the benefit of your former tenants, since they're the ones who've paid such a high price for your utter negligence and incompetence.

"You will also be stripped of your title, and you will be required to do community service to help those you have so badly wronged. Do you have anything to say?"

"No," said the former Lord Upworth.

"Henceforth you'll be known simply as Robert. We will see to it that you get enough income from your lands to support your family modestly. You will be instructed in how to farm your lands here in the capital, and farm them you will. In time, maybe you'll change your ways and learn some humility and compassion."

"Yes, Your Majesty."

"You may go now. You will receive the appropriate legal documents to-morrow, but meanwhile, walk carefully and do penance for those twenty-three dead children."

Robert stood, shoulders hunched, looking like a broken man, and left.

Once he was gone, Ty said, "So where is Johnston? Who was the mes-senger? And where did the money come from? I suspect even Lord Upworth would have noticed if six chests of money had been stolen from him. That couldn't all have been his."

"Good point and good questions," said King Bertram. "We must con-tinue to investigate."

"Sapphira and Magnolia met with Criseda and me this morning and made it very clear that The Wraith has them worried. They have no idea who he is, but they're saying that his minions are to be found all through Estrea, and they warned me to watch my back even in Dragonwind," said Ty.

"That's very disquieting," said Bertram.

"They also said that Esme is especially important to our planet, so I'm making her safety my number one priority. That being said, her safety is de-pendent on catching The Wraith, so I'll be hunting him as well."

"I'll see what can be done from here," said Bertram. "Whoever it is, it obviously isn't the former Lord Upworth. I'll look into Lord Goforth as his lands lie south of here, nowhere near Dragonwind."

"Just be careful," said Ty. "Also, Wilhelmina is a very powerful telepath, and she can speak from Dragonwind directly to you. I know the fox network has been great, but I have to admit that knowing I can reach you directly or that you can reach me, using Wilhelmina, is a big relief."

"That will help," said Bertram.

"Criseda and I had better get back to Dragonwind," said Ty. "But if you need us, or if you learn anything, just call for Wilhelmina. She'll hear you. I'm beginning to wonder how I ever managed without her. And her devotion to Paul is incredible. She's even taught him telepathy. The dragons have the greatest respect for her, and I can certainly understand why."

"That's wonderful," said Bertram. "I've authorized a large shipment of food, blankets, and clothing, and even some building supplies, to be sent to Dragonwind to help with your increased population. If you need anything else, just let me know."

"Thank you, sir," said Ty. "Watch your own back. Talk with you soon."

With that, Ty went out into the courtyard and vaulted onto Criseda.

CHAPTER 13

NIGHTTIME RAIDS

Ty and Criseda reached Ty's home, and Ty realized just how tired he was after the past few days. Before making his dinner and then heading to bed, Ty checked in with Wilhelmina, who reported that everything was quiet. A good night's sleep was certainly in order.

Unfortunately, it wasn't to be. In the middle of the night, Esme woke screaming from a nightmare. Wilhelmina immediately contacted Ty. *I'm sorry to wake you, but I think we need to take this seriously.*

Ty rubbed his eyes and sat up in bed before responding. *Have any of our watchers reported anything?*

Wilhelmina answered, *Not so far, but I've asked Miranda and Mirabella to search Dragonwind. Remember, the dragons said we could have some of The Wraith's henchmen in Dragonwind. That would explain why nobody's been seen approaching on the road.*

True, said Ty. *Criseda and I will be right there.*

Ty and Criseda arrived on the village green five minutes later. Criseda walked around Dragonwind while Ty went to Martha's to talk with Esme. He found her sitting at Martha's kitchen table, a mug of hot chocolate in front of her, Rupert in her lap, and Samantha sitting on the kitchen table next to her. Esme was as white as a sheet, and her hands were shaking. Martha sat next to her with her right arm around Esme's shoulders.

Ty sat down across from her and said, in a quiet, gentle voice, "Esme, can you tell me what you sensed?"

Esme nodded slowly. "I can still feel it. There's an evil presence here in Dragonwind—a very strong evil presence that I haven't felt since I escaped from my parents."

"Is it your parents?" asked Ty.

Esme shook her head. "No, it isn't them. They're very bad people who've made some horrible choices, but they aren't truly evil. This presence is just that, truly evil and very powerful. My parents are bullies, but they're weak. No, this is very different."

Ty thought for a few minutes. "Have you felt this presence before? Either at your parents' home or here in Dragonwind?"

Esme looked terrified as she nodded. "Only when The Wraith visited my parents. And this is the first time here in Dragonwind. I would have told you immediately if I'd felt it again here."

Ty looked at Martha and saw the worry etched on her face, knowing full well that the same worry must be reflected on his own face. He turned back to Esme. "I know we've asked some of these questions before, but have you ever seen The Wraith? Even a brief glimpse? Or a partial view of him? Have you heard his voice?"

Esme shook her head miserably. "No, never. Remember, I was locked in my tiny bedroom. And now, that's weird: I realize that he never spoke to my parents. How is that possible?"

This piqued Ty's interest. "Was The Wraith alone when he came? Did he come often?"

"He only came once or twice that I remember," said Esme. "And he had one of his henchmen with him. It was the henchman who spoke, not The Wraith."

"OK," said Ty. "Did you ever see the henchman? Did he come more often than The Wraith?"

Esme nodded. "There were several different henchmen, and they would come every week or two to get information out of my parents. I couldn't see them, but I did hear them. And I could read the men's minds, but all I got from them was terror. They were as scared as my parents."

Just then Miranda called to Ty. *We saw two men trying to get into the barn, but then they saw Wilhelmina, and they took off running.*

Thanks, Miranda.

Ty turned to Esme again. "Do you still sense the evil?"

Esme was quiet for a few minutes. Then she shook her head and said, with obvious relief in her voice, "No, it's gone."

Martha let out a big sigh of relief. "Then maybe we should get you back into bed. You'll have Rupert and Samantha with you, and Wilhelmina and Criseda, along with Miranda and Mirabella, will be on guard outside."

Esme finished her hot chocolate and stood up, and Martha took her, along with Rupert and Samantha, back to Esme's bedroom. When she returned, she looked at Ty. "What do you think?"

"I honestly don't know what to think," answered Ty. "The Wraith doesn't seem like anything we've ever come across before. I'm not sure he's even human. Or is he just really good at keeping his identity secret and hiding his appearance?"

"How did he get here, and how did he leave?" asked Martha.

"No idea," said Ty. "The two men who ran off are probably henchmen, but Esme wouldn't have felt evil from them. I suspect she'd say the same thing about them as she did about her parents—bad men, no doubt bullies, who weren't too bright. Interesting that she said the henchmen were terrified. I have no doubt that whoever or whatever The Wraith is, he or it was here tonight."

"Why?" asked Martha, "And if The Wraith is so powerful, why hasn't he just snatched Esme?"

"That is a very interesting question, and I suspect if we could answer it, we'd know a lot more about him," said Ty. "The Wraith obviously has some supernatural powers, but since he can't just take Esme, he also has limitations. He relies on his henchmen for any physical work."

"How will you be able to figure out what or who he is?" asked Martha.

"I'm not sure," said Ty, "but tomorrow I'm going to talk to Sapphire again. I'm hoping that the dragons might have some ideas about this."

"Well, it's obvious you and King Bertram were right that it isn't the former Lord Upworth, and it probably isn't any of the other suspects either. I sure hope you can solve the mystery and find a solution before anyone is hurt."

"Me too," said Ty. Then he called to Wilhelmina. *Do you think that's all the excitement for tonight?*

Yes, but I'll keep watch just to be sure.

Thanks. Then Ty said to Martha, "Criseda and I are going home for now. Wilhelmina can get us if needed, but I do need some sleep, and I need to ponder all this. In the morning, I'm going to talk with the dragons and then I'll be back."

Ty gave Martha a big hug. "Take care of yourself."

Martha answered, "You too."

CHAPTER 14

SAFETY MEASURES

Ty went down to Dragonwind in the morning to be there when the convoy of supplies arrived from King Bertram. He was pleased to see that the majority of the villagers, as well as the newly arrived refugees, were there. As King Bertram's men unloaded the three wagons, Ty announced that the king was very grateful to Dragonwind for helping those who'd been left homeless and that he would provide assistance for them so that their support, while they were getting back on their feet, wouldn't be a burden on the residents of Dragonwind.

The villagers cheered for the king, but Ty noticed that Drake and two other men looked mutinous. It was going to be much harder for them to sow discontent if the villagers were receiving the king's assistance.

Ty continued. "I have also received permission to make land grants to any of the new families looking to stay here in Dragonwind. As you know, I was left in charge of lands confiscated from the traitor Lord Osterfels. Some of you have already received holdings; those who didn't have land of their own. Now you will have some more neighbors. I know that Wilson and his family wish to remain with us, and we're most fortunate to have such a talented carpenter to add to our list of craftsmen. Furthermore, in addition to building his own home, he's offered to help build homes for any of the new refugees who would like assistance."

"What do we need with a bunch of widows with no talent?" shouted someone from the back, and Ty was quite certain it was Drake.

Ty said, "All are welcome in Dragonwind. Of the twenty-seven refugees who arrived right after Wilson and his family, two of the men and seven of the women, with their children, have already been assisted to head to the capital where they have family. The remaining refugees are most welcome here."

"Says you," shouted another man. "You, the freak; you, the girl who thinks she's a man—"

But before he could say anymore, the villagers started booing him, shouting him down. Someone said, "Ty's done more for us than anyone else, certainly more than you miserable excuses for men."

Before things could get truly ugly, Ty held up his hands and asked for quiet. Then he said, "You don't have to like me. You don't have to agree with me. But I have been given charge of the well-being of all in Dragonwind, and I will carry out that mandate as long as it is mine. You are able bodied, and no one is forcing you to remain here. If you don't like how things are run, and I think it's quite obvious from this gathering that you are in the minority, then you are free to move on. No one is telling you how to live or forcing you to do something you don't want. We're looking after our own, both current and new villagers, and if you have a problem with that, take it up with the king."

"Ha," said Drake, now stepping forward so that he could be seen by all. "You think you have it made, but let me tell you, I know the king won't be around for much longer. There's going to be a new power in Estrea, and it won't take kindly to weak freaks."

With that, Drake turned and left, followed by two other men. There was an uneasy silence as the men disappeared into the forest.

Miranda, can you and your friends follow them?

We're on it, Ty.

Thanks.

Jeb, who was nearby, looked at Ty and then motioned toward Drake, indicating that he also would follow the men. Ty nodded and mouthed, "Thanks."

Ty then addressed the village. "Well, there's no way to please everyone."

That brought a chuckle, and the mood lightened.

Ty said, "We have plenty here for everyone. Martha and Kyle will help with the distribution. There is clothing, and I hope I gave King Bertram the right information about sizes. If not, those of you who can sew will be able, I'm sure, to fix things. We have food, so if you're one of the hosting families, be sure you take enough for your own family as well as for the guests you're housing. And finally, there are building supplies, which we can store until they are needed. I know Wilson is eager to get going on his home, so we'll send his to the spot he's picked out. We'll do the same for the rest of you whenever you're ready. Welcome one and all to Dragonwind."

There was loud, thunderous applause as Ty stepped away from the carts. Then Martha and Kyle moved forward to beginning distributing the supplies.

Ty headed to Martha's barn. He really needed to talk with Wilhelmina. Drake's outburst had him truly worried now.

He walked into the barn and smiled when he saw Esme and Paul playing and laughing, with Rupert, Samantha, and Wilhelmina looking on. He couldn't help but wonder what lay ahead for the two of them, but for now, they were happy.

Wilhelmina, did you hear Drake?

Yes, I did, Wilhelmina replied. *His speech is worrying. I'll pass it along to King Bertram, if you want.*

Please, said Ty. *I don't know if The Wraith put Drake up to it, or if Drake just lost his head, but it does sound as if the threat to Estrea is serious. This isn't some petty crook, but then I guess we knew that.*

Are you going to meet with Sapphire? asked Wilhelmina.

Yes, said Ty, *I'm heading up there now. I sure hope they know something.*

Good luck, and I'll keep an eye on things here, especially these two.

Thanks, Wilhelmina, said Ty as he left the barn and hiked back up the mountain to the dragons' aerie.

Sapphire and Magnolia were waiting for him when he reached the meeting place.

Good morning, Ty. You're really worried, and I'm afraid you have good reason to be.

Hi, Sapphire. Can you help? I'm not sure who or even what The Wraith is. Do you have any ideas?

We've been searching our records, said Magnolia. *Centuries ago there were tales of an evil presence in the mountains where the mines were. We don't know anything about the evil, or indeed if it was even real. It seemed to exist for a few years and then it disappeared—or at least there were no more tales about it.*

Tell me honestly, said Ty, *do you think we're dealing with something human or something supernatural?*

Sapphire shook her head. *Frankly, we don't know. But we're determined to find out. Our records predate the human settlements in this area, so in some ways, this is our problem. But Drake's outburst this morning—and yes, we were listening to your meeting—have raised the threat level. I think we need to do several things.*

First, Sapphire continued, *we need to offer sanctuary to Esme and Paul, and that needs to happen today. And yes, we can include not only Rupert and Samantha but also Wilhelmina. We'll work out the details, but we need to ensure their safety.*

Also, I'd like to send Oscar and Foster to King Bertram, to keep watch on him and the capital. He's the best king this nation has ever seen, which is going to make him a target for this evil, no matter what kind of evil it is. Having Oscar and Foster in the capital will also facilitate communication between King Bertram and you.

Ty thought about Sapphire's proposal. *I think your plans are sensible. We can't guarantee Esme and Paul's safety in Dragonwind, and King Bertram could use extra protection. I'll ask Criseda to help me transport Esme and Paul up here now.*

Sapphire nodded. *We will watch over your young ones. They are important to all of us.*

Ty stood and called to Criseda. *Can you help me bring Esme, Rupert, Samantha, Paul, and Wilhelmina here?*

Criseda came into the meeting circle. *Of course, but I think Wilhelmina will be happier getting here on her own.*

Ty laughed. *That's for sure. I can't imagine she'd like to be dangled from your claws. Maybe Martha could come with her, as I'm sure Martha would like to see Esme and Paul settled.* Then he quickly added, *Not that we don't think you guys will do a great job. Still, I think she'd feel better if she saw for herself. It's going to be hard on Paul's mother, Naomi, but I don't think we can let her come with Paul.*

Sapphire said, *Martha's most welcome and she can, of course, visit them anytime she wants. She has done nothing but care for them, giving her all to their healing. Martha is amazing, for a human. However, I agree about Naomi. We don't think she's involved, but we need the fewest number of humans possible coming and going. Our aerie is secure, but a concentrated assault would cause injuries. No sense in taking chances.*

Ty nodded before he vaulted onto Criseda, and the two of them flew down to Dragonwind.

Martha wasn't very happy when she heard that Esme and Paul needed to be moved, but she understood. "Their safety has to be the primary consideration," she said, "but I'll miss them."

"Hopefully it won't be for forever," said Ty. "And the dragons did say you could visit anytime. I'm sure Criseda would take you whenever you want."

"Oh my," said Martha. "That's a daunting prospect. I've never ridden a dragon."

Ty chuckled. "I'm sure you'd love it. But for now, Criseda is going to take Esme, Rupert, Samantha, and Paul. I told the dragons that you'd want to get them settled, so if Wilhelmina is willing," Ty paused to look at the moose, "then you can ride her along with whatever bedding and supplies you think you'll need to settle them. I'll ride White Star, and we can take more things if needed."

"How will they eat? Do dragons know how to fix human food?" Martha asked.

"I'm sure they'll manage just fine. Remember, I lived with the dragons after I was nearly killed, and I did well," said Ty.

"But Kyle was with you," protested Martha.

"Not all the time," said Ty. "If you're really worried, maybe Kyle would be willing to stay with them. I could check with Sapphire. That way you wouldn't have to close your bakery."

"This is a lot to take in," said Martha. "I suppose the first thing is just to get the kids up to the dragons so that they have sanctuary. One step at a time."

"That's the idea. Now I'm going out to the barn to tell Esme and Paul and to get them onto Criseda. The sooner they're out of Dragonwind, the safer they'll be."

Martha said, "I don't think Naomi is going to be thrilled about this. She spends all her time with Paul. It will be very hard on her to be separated again."

"I know," said Ty, "but the dragons don't want anymore humans than necessary. Maybe you could encourage Naomi to start working on a proper home for her, Paul, and Wilhelmina and help her figure out what she can do to earn her way. That is, if she's planning to keep them in Dragonwind."

"She is, and you're right," said Martha. "Planning their future will give her something to do, and I'll help her as well as the other widows who've elected to stay."

Ty left Martha's kitchen and went into the barn. "You guys want to go live with the dragons?" he said as he entered.

"Wow," said Esme.

"For real?" said Paul.

"Yep," said Ty. "And Criseda is going to take you there right now."

"What about Rupert and Samantha?" said Esme.

"And Wilhelmina?" said Paul.

"Not to worry," said Ty. "Rupert and Samantha will ride with you two. Wilhelmina would not be happy being carried by a dragon."

I certainly would not! said Wilhelmina firmly.

Ty nodded. "Wilhelmina will make her own way up, as will White Star with me. If Wilhelmina is willing, Martha will ride with her on the way up, and then once she's satisfied that you two have proper accommodations, she'll come back down on White Star."

I'd be happy to bring Martha up, said Wilhelmina.

Thanks, said Ty. He turned to Esme and Paul. "Grab whatever you need right now, including warm coats. I'll help the four of you onto Criseda. Then I'll help Martha pack everything else you might need, and knowing Martha, that will be lots. We'll see you once we get up there, but you'll be fine with Criseda. You know her."

"OK," said Paul, "I guess. But Wilhelmina is coming, right?"

"Definitely," said Ty.

98

I'll be there as quickly as I can, said Wilhelmina. *And we can talk all the way. You'll never be out of communication range. So please don't worry. You'll be much safer with the dragons. No one will be able to hurt you there.*

"That's the plan. Now come on, Esme," Ty said as he bent down to pick up Paul.

Rupert and Samantha followed them out into the courtyard, and Ty placed Paul on top of Criseda, followed by Esme. Then he lifted Rupert, who sat in front of Esme, her arms around him. Finally, he lifted Samantha, who cuddled with Paul.

Once Ty was sure everyone was seated securely, he took a big heavy blanket and wrapped it around them all. Criseda said, *I'll take good care of them.*

And with that, she took off for the dragons' aerie. It wasn't more than ten minutes before Criseda said, *They're all here, safe and sound, and Sapphire is settling them into an unused dragon cave.*

Thanks, Criseda. Martha, Wilhelmina, and I should be setting out in about a half hour. That will get us to you before dark.

Martha was bustling around, packing clothes—especially extra warm ones—for Esme and Paul, more blankets and pillows, their favorite toys, and a lot of food, including a big pot of stew.

Ty was kept busy packing everything into bundles that Wilhelmina and White Star could carry. Kyle helped with the packing and then asked, "When will you come back down?"

Before Martha could answer, Ty said, "White Star and I will bring her down tonight."

"But I might need to stay longer," said Martha.

"Martha, they'll be just fine. Wilhelmina or Criseda will let us know if they need anything. The dragons are doing us a huge favor by keeping them, but remember, the aerie is the dragons' home, and they aren't used to humans. We need to respect their space. They've promised to care for Esme and Paul, and believe me, they will take great care of them. Sapphire thinks both of them, but especially Esme, are important to the survival of the planet, so they won't let anything happen to them."

"OK," said Martha, a bit tentatively. "If you say so."

"I do, so let's get going," said Ty.

Kyle helped Martha onto Wilhelmina's back, and then he and Ty lashed the last of Martha's bundles onto White Star. Ty mounted the horse, and they started off.

Darkness was just beginning to fall as White Star and Wilhelmina walked into the center of the aerie. Ty dismounted and helped Martha off Wilhelmina. Then Criseda showed them to the cave Esme, Rupert, Samantha, and Paul were using. It was large enough for Wilhelmina to enter, which thrilled Paul. While Martha looked around the space and checked that everything was going to work, Ty unloaded first Wilhelmina, who'd come into the cave, bags and all, and then White Star. He helped Martha store everything neatly. Criseda showed Martha the firepit where her stew pot could be placed, and Criseda promised to heat the stew for Esme and Paul.

Finally, Ty had to insist that Martha say good night to the kids, as they still had to get back down to Dragonwind. Reluctantly, she agreed, and after giving both Paul and Esme hugs, Martha let Ty help her onto White Star, and the three of them left, promising that they would check in with Wilhelmina in the morning.

CHAPTER 15

SCOUTING REPORTS

The next morning, Ty was getting breakfast for himself and Foxy when Jeb arrived. He was breathless and looked exhausted. Ty said, "Come on in, and I'll fix you some breakfast."

"Thanks," said Jeb, as he dug into a plate of scrambled eggs. Once he'd finished, he said, "I followed Drake and his friends. Miranda and Mirabella are still watching them, but I came back to report. Drake sounded pretty cocky at the village green, but once he got to his cabin, I heard him talking with his friends, and they sounded scared."

"What did they say?" asked Ty.

"It seems they were supposed to kidnap Esme last night, when we found them sniffing around. Drake said that their 'boss' was not going to be happy that they'd failed. Apparently the boss, whoever that is, doesn't take kindly to failures."

"I see," said Ty. "Anything else?"

"Yes," said Jeb. "It seems they know Johnston, and they're now really concerned because they're pretty sure Johnston has been murdered. They haven't found his body or anything, but they also haven't seen him, and he was supposed to meet with them a few days ago. Now they're worried that they'll be the next casualties, since you've put Esme out of their reach. They may not be bright, but they know what would happen to them if they tried to get her from the dragons' home."

"Did you find out how The Wraith, who I assume is their boss, communicates with them?" asked Ty.

Jeb shook his head. "No, I didn't hear anything about that. Right now, they're so scared they're staying inside Drake's cabin and not moving."

"Hmm," said Ty. "I wonder. Do you think they're at all likely to turn on their boss?"

"I'd say no," said Jeb. "They seem to be terrified of him. They already think that Johnston was murdered, and they're afraid they're next in line. They also don't think that anyone can stop their boss. They mentioned again that even the king won't be able to stop him."

"I sure wish I knew more about The Wraith," said Ty. "We don't even know if he's human or magical. We know nothing, but when Esme described the evil she felt when he was near, it really worried me. I know it's got the dragons concerned too, and anything that worries dragons is not something I want to mess with."

"At one point, Drake said something about the boss hiding behind a black, hooded cloak, but I don't know that that helps much," said Jeb. "Well, I'd better get back and keep watch."

Jeb stood up and started toward the cave door. Ty went with him, and as his friend left, Ty said, "Please be really careful. All of you. And get out of there if there's the slightest danger. I don't want to lose you."

"I will," said Jeb. "Trust me, I don't want to end up murdered."

Once Jeb had gone, Ty sat at his kitchen table drinking his tea and going over everything they'd figured out. It sure wasn't much. The hard part was that Ty had no idea how to find out more.

Wilhelmina contacted him. *Esme and Paul are enjoying their stay with the dragons.*

That's good news, said Ty. *I'm guessing that they'll be there for a while. I have no idea what to do next. I don't even know where to look for information.*

The dragons are searching their archives, but so far, they've not come up with anything, said Wilhelmina. *It was so long ago that there was anything like this evil, and not many records from that time still exist. And there don't seem to be any clues as to the identity of the evil or how it was defeated.*

Ty groaned. *And the dragons have the oldest records. How are we going to defeat this thing, whatever it is?*

I don't know, said Wilhelmina. *However, I suspect that whatever it is, it feeds off fear and hate. If that's the case, it won't be defeated by force.*

You mean that we can't battle it? said Ty.

That's just what I mean, said Wilhelmina. *We're going to have to defeat it by denying it power over us, by not fearing it, by not turning on one another. I'm not sure, but that's just my gut instinct.*

I'll give that some serious thought, said Ty. *Can you share your thoughts with Sapphire and Magnolia and see what they think?*

Sure thing. And please let Martha and Naomi know that we're all doing well here. The dragons are teaching Esme and Paul, and I'm enjoying watching them learn. Esme, of course, has tremendous magical abilities, and I thought Paul had only what I helped him get—telepathy with me—but it seems I wasn't as clever as I thought, or I should say, that he has some natural abilities that I just awakened. I don't know how far he'll go, but it's fun to watch him expand his abilities.

Ty chuckled. *I'll pass on your news to Martha and Naomi. Talk with you later.*

Ty hiked down to Dragonwind to check on things there. He stopped first at Martha's and passed along Wilhelmina's message to both Martha and Naomi.

Naomi said, "I miss Paul. Is he really in danger?"

Ty said, "We just don't want to take any chances. Esme is certainly in danger. Several attempts have already been made on her life. Paul may not be in danger, but he does have knowledge that the villains are trying to keep hidden, so I'd rather be safe than sorry."

Naomi nodded. "Thank you for looking after him."

Martha patted Naomi's shoulder. "I bet he's having the time of his life staying with dragons. Not many people get to do that. He'll have so many stories to tell you when he returns."

Naomi smiled. "And this time, I'll believe him. I still feel badly that I thought he was making up his ability to talk with Wilhelmina."

"I'm sure he understands," said Ty. "Telepathic gifts are extremely rare, so there was no reason for you to even know they existed."

Martha changed the subject. "We're trying to figure out what the women who want to stay in Dragonwind can do to earn their living. And we're working on getting small cottages built for them."

"That's an excellent plan," said Ty.

"I want to have a nice home for Paul to come back to," said Naomi. "Everyone here is so kind. I know we'll make a good life here."

Martha said, "The refugees want to make a positive contribution after all the kindness they've received. They've noticed that we don't have a tea shop or small café, or even a proper community center where folks can come together. There's a vacant lot next to my bakery on the south side, as you know, and Wilson is thinking that something could be built there. Then the women could run it as a tea shop. It would give Dragonwind something new and it would also be an enterprise that the women are well qualified to administer."

"That sounds like an excellent plan," said Ty. "I for one would love to have somewhere to stop for lunch or a late-afternoon tea. I can cook, but it's not my favorite activity, and it's definitely harder to cook for just one. I say go for it if that's what the refugees want to do. It would most assuredly be appreciated by the entire village."

"Thanks, Ty," said Martha. "I'll let them know, and we'll get Wilson to plan something."

Ty stood. "I need to leave now. Criseda and I are going to fly to the palace. After Drake's outburst yesterday, I need to talk with King Bertram."

On their way to the palace, they passed a crevasse where they saw a flock of vultures. Ty said, *I think we need to investigate that.*

Criseda found a relatively level spot along the path to land. Her arrival caused the vultures to fly off, screaming in anger. Ty walked toward the spot where they'd been, and he found a man's body, lying facedown. Ty turned it over and saw that it was Johnston. However, the look of absolute terror on his face startled Ty. He could find no wounds to account for the death, and as he and Criseda searched the area, they found evidence that someone, probably Johnston, had been running and sliding along the downward sloping path. Then Johnston's footprints seemed to slide right off the cliff.

Ty said, *It looks as if he was running away from something. That he thought something was after him. If it was dark, he might have missed the curve in the path and simply run off the cliff.*

Criseda nodded in agreement. *His body looks as if he was killed by the fall. So there wasn't a murder. At least it doesn't appear to have been. Instead, he was frightened to death.*

Ty looked worried. *I think I would have preferred murder. Johnston didn't strike me as the kind of man to be easily scared, but the look on his face is one of absolute terror.*

They searched some more but could gain no additional information. Ty said, *Can you dig a grave here, in the crevasse? Is there enough space? I don't really want to leave him for the vultures.*

He was going to let Paul and the others die in the mines, said Criseda. *And he did allow all those others to be killed. Maybe vultures are a fitting end for him.*

Ty said, *I will treat his body with respect for our sake, not his. We will not stoop to the level of our enemies.*

Criseda examined the crevasse. *I can make a rockslide that will cover his body. That would be the easiest, and it would also make the path a bit safer here.*

Ty nodded. *That's an excellent idea. Then some good will come of this sorry end.*

Once they'd buried Johnston, they resumed their flight.

Ty and Criseda arrived in the palace's central courtyard to find Foster and Oscar on guard duty.

Things have been really quiet, Foster reported.

Boring, said Oscar, who was a young dragon, younger even than Criseda.

There's a lot to be said for boring, said Foster.

Oscar didn't look convinced. Ty thanked them both and headed into the palace. Henry took him immediately to see King Bertram.

After exchanging greetings, King Bertram said, "Foster and Oscar have made an impression on the palace population. My sons are thrilled to meet them. But are they really necessary?"

"I gather Wilhelmina told you about Drake's threats," said Ty.

"Yes, she did, but still," said Bertram.

"Sapphire doesn't want to take any chances," said Ty. "We have no idea what this threat is, but it's more than anything this world has ever seen. Or at least more than this world has seen since people have lived here. And trust me, the look on Johnston's face was one that I hope never to see again. Whatever is threatening us is a very real evil."

Ty went on to explain the little bit that they'd managed to learn from the ancient dragon archives.

King Bertram looked thoughtful at this news. "I can see why Sapphire is worried. The palace has some old historical archives, but not as old as the dragons' records. Still, I wonder if Aloysius could shed some light on this. He knows the palace archives better than anyone. I'll ask Henry to see if he's willing to come down from his tower. He practically lives in the archives."

Ty said, "I think it might be better if we went to Aloysius. I remember him well, and he gets cranky if he isn't in his space. Also, he might want to consult references."

"That's true," said Bertram. "OK, let's go see him."

They headed out of Bertram's office and walked along several hallways until they came to a narrow spiral staircase that led up to the tallest round turret in the palace.

CHAPTER 16

HISTORICAL ARCHIVES

After he and Ty had climbed up the four flights of stairs in the circular stairway, King Bertram knocked on the door of the archives and then walked in. Aloysius was sitting on a tall stool, hunched over an ancient manuscript. He looked up, peering over the top of his wire-framed spectacles.

"Your Majesty," he said. "What brings you all the way up here?"

King Bertram smiled at the ancient historian. "We need to pick your brain and have you search the oldest archives, and somehow we thought you'd prefer us to come to you."

"Ah," said Aloysius, "you know me well. I don't like to leave my tower. What's troubling you?"

Ty quickly summarized the little they'd discovered about The Wraith. "The dragons have archives that are much older than any human records, but they can't find anything of substance. They've found references to a horrible evil that tried to overtake the entire planet, and then later a note that the evil had been destroyed, but there were no indications as to what the evil was or how it was defeated."

"We also," said King Bertram, "don't know if this so-called Wraith is the same evil or something entirely different."

Ty nodded. "We have no idea how it's communicating with its minions. We don't even know what The Wraith is, but we have a young girl, Esme, with extraordinary magical powers and sensitivities who says it's pure evil, whether human or magical, or some combination. She says it goes well beyond what bad men normally do."

Aloysius began shifting documents, searching for something. "I've been studying some ancient references to even more ancient legends. I hadn't put much credence in them, but now, with what you're saying, I'm wondering if maybe there isn't some truth in these legends.

"You know that there are plenty of tales we tell our children to scare them into being good. Those tales aren't history or anything we'd begin to call truth. They just are, with no known author or beginning. And they've changed shape over the centuries. But it's my belief that there was a past event or happening that forms the underlying basis for each of the tales."

Ty said, "That makes sense. Something served as the inspiration for the tale and then the person who made up the tale just embellished on that."

"Precisely," said Aloysius. "Well, I've found an ancient and obscure reference to a village that was plagued by an evil spirit. Just a minute; I know I can find it here somewhere."

Aloysius began moving scrolls around, shifting piles of materials, putting some things on the floor, and picking up other piles. Ty and Bertram looked on as the old man seemed to make a bigger mess of things than he already had, but finally, he pulled one scroll out and set it down in front of him. "Here, this is what I wanted."

He spoke as he unrolled the scroll. "One of our most learned philosophers, Tobias, who lived centuries ago, recorded all the ancient legends he could find. He spent a lifetime studying them, and he came to some conclusions, which, to be honest, I thought were pretty outlandish, but now I'm wondering if I was too hasty.

"He felt that the tales about evil beings were based in fact, that things had happened in the far-distant past that gave rise to these tales. I don't know if he had any access to the dragons' archives, but if you say they also talk of an unspeakable evil, I have to conclude that there was some basis for these tales."

Ty asked, "Did Tobias have any idea how to combat the evil? Or where it came from?"

Aloysius said, "As far as where it came from, it invariably evolved from deep within the ground. I always figured that was because people are buried, and we generally don't want to go deep into the earth, so it was just a convenient location, much like saying goodness comes from the sky."

"However," said King Bertram, "the stories of The Wraith started to appear after Lord Upworth had dug his mines to new depths, and then the veins of ore and minerals petered out."

"Interesting," said Aloysius as he began jotting notes to himself. "Then as far as defeating the evil, well, I'm afraid that gets a lot more fanciful and inexplicable. I just thought they were happily-ever-after stories for children. The evil was defeated by love, happiness, joy, and other such things. It could never be defeated by fighting, and the more people feared or hated, the stronger the evil became."

Ty got excited. "That's what Wilhelmina said. She has a gut feeling that fighting will only make things worse."

Aloysius said, "Who's Wilhelmina?"

It took Ty a few minutes to explain and even more to convince Aloysius that telepathy and magic were real. Finally, Aloysius said, "Well, I have a lot to learn, more than I ever realized. I need to study everything Tobias ever wrote."

King Bertram said, "Please make that your highest priority, as the threat from whatever The Wraith might be is very real and very menacing."

"Certainly, Your Majesty," said Aloysius. "You should also know that in all the stories, there is always a hero who brings about the defeat. That is probably just a story convention to give the tales more punch, but still. There's so much of this that I never thought was anything more than a good story, or in some cases a very far-fetched story, but now I'm beginning to see that they might hold some real truths.

"Tobias said, for instance, that all of life is made up of various vibrations that interact with one another. He uses this as proof that all life is connected and that our very thoughts produce our realities. I need to study this more, but that might help explain how something like fear could bring something to life, or make it stronger if it sprang from somewhere else, like the bottom of a mine. Oh dear, there are more possibilities than I can fathom at the moment."

King Bertram put a hand on the old man's shoulder. "Take a deep breath. We do need you to work on this and work quickly, but we don't need to panic. Study whatever you can find. Ty will take this information to the dragons, who will also be helping. If you come up with any ideas, no matter how far-fetched you may think them to be, bring them to me, and I'll pass them on to Ty and the dragons."

Aloysius took a deep breath and nodded. "I'll do all I can, Your Majesty. You know, I've never thought that anyone would be interested in my research. Oh, I know I taught your father history, and then you, and now your children, and I know the history of Estrea and the other nations is important, but from what you're telling me now, what I learn from Tobias could save our planet. That's quite a responsibility."

"Yes, it is," said the king, "but it isn't yours alone. We're all in this. What did Tobias say? We're all connected. I think we're going to learn a lot about those connections."

Ty and King Bertram turned to leave. They looked back as they opened the door to find Aloysius once again moving piles and piles of scrolls. Ty couldn't help but say, "I wonder if there's any organization to his system."

King Bertram laughed as they headed down the spiral stairs. "I don't know, but he did manage to find what he was looking for pretty quickly. I suspect he knows where everything is, and if anyone were ever rash enough to try to straighten up his space, he'd lose everything."

"I suppose," said Ty. "He's certainly given us a lot to think about. My brain feels as if it's been twisted in a knot."

"I agree," said the king. "I guess for now we just try to keep everyone safe and stop the regular villains like Johnston, Drake and his friends, and Esme's parents. I can't say that I'm sorry Johnston is dead, but the manner of his death is troubling. As far as I know, Esme's parents are still living in their home, but I think I'd better send someone to keep an eye on them."

"That's a good idea," said Ty, "and Jeb, along with Miranda and Mirabella, are keeping an eye on Drake and company."

When they'd reached the main floor of the palace, Ty said, "I'll keep in contact with you. I think Criseda and I need to talk with Wilhelmina and the dragons."

"I agree," said the king. "Stay safe."

"You too," said Ty. He headed out into the courtyard and said goodbye to Oscar and Foster, and then he and Criseda headed back to Dragonwind.

CHAPTER 17

DRAGON LESSONS

Esme and Paul were seated on a stone bench on the edge of the dragons' firepit. Rupert and Samantha sat close to Esme, and Wilhelmina stood behind Paul. Sapphire and Magnolia were on the other side of the pit, ready to begin another day of lessons. Esme had never imagined there was so much to learn. She was very glad that Elfrida had taught her to read and write. The dragon lessons were much more intense. They were more philosophical—at least that was the word Sapphire had used.

Esme wasn't entirely sure what that meant, but they were learning about history: the history of the dragons, the history of the humans in Estrea, and the relationships between Estrea and the other nations of this world, especially the neighboring nation of Mlinred, which had always had turbulent relations with Estrea.

In addition to history, Sapphire was teaching them about human interactions: friendships, hatreds, and how emotions worked. Sapphire was very gentle with her and Paul. They both knew that they were fortunate to have Sapphire and Magnolia teaching them and that they were getting an education unlike anyone else had ever received.

Sapphire said, *So how do you deal with someone who doesn't like you?*

Paul answered first. "I usually just try to stay away from them."

Esme said, "I don't really know, as I've never had any contact with people my own age. The only ones I had contact with were my parents, and while they didn't much like me, they needed something from me, something I didn't want to give them, so I just tried to be as quiet as I could be and hoped I'd turn invisible."

Sapphire nodded. *Both of your reactions are perfectly normal. But we're never going to be liked by everyone, just as we'll never like everyone. However, we need to learn to get along, to show respect for others even when we disagree.*

Paul said, "What do we do if they hit us?"

Sapphire knew from the look on his young face that he'd experienced this and that he'd suffered from the attention of bullies. *If you are being hurt, you need to find an adult who will protect you. Under no circumstance should you abandon yourself. You have a right to be treated fairly.*

Magnolia said, *Do you know that those who've suffered from bullying and abuse all too often become bullies and abusers themselves when they're older? Why do you suppose that is?*

Esme said, very quietly, "Maybe because that's all they know. Maybe because they want some payback for all they've suffered. Maybe because they don't know any other way to be."

Magnolia smiled. *Unfortunately, all those reasons are present. So for you, especially, Esme, and yes also for you, Paul, you need to learn better, more effective ways to handle conflict. Tell me, do you think fighting solves problems?*

Esme and Paul were both quiet. Finally, Paul said, "It's worked to make me do stuff, when someone bigger and stronger forced me to do what they wanted."

Esme nodded in agreement.

But how does that make you feel? asked Sapphire. *Is it effective?*

Esme thought and finally said, "It worked in the short term. But then I resented those who had forced me to do what I didn't want, and all I could think of was how to get back at them."

Precisely, said Sapphire. *In the long run, force and violence are not solutions. They just add to the problems.*

While Esme and Paul were thinking about this, Ty and Criseda landed in the clearing next to the firepit. They came over, and Ty said, *I really need to talk with you, Sapphire. I've learned something from the ancient archives at the palace.*

Sapphire pointed to the bench next to Esme and Paul. *Have a seat and join our lessons. I think we all need to hear from you.*

Ty looked over at Esme and Paul and then back to Sapphire. *Are you sure? They're so young.* Ty kept his thoughts focused and shielded so that only Sapphire and Magnolia heard him.

Sapphire answered him, also shielding her thoughts from Esme and Paul. *I'm sure. I think we're going to need these two.*

Ty sat down on a bench. "I worked with King Bertram and Aloysius, the palace historian, in discussing the writings of an ancient philosopher named Tobias.

"Tobias talks about how everything in the world has vibrations and that those vibrations are somehow connected. I don't exactly understand what he's saying, but it would seem that everything is connected, some more closely and some more distantly. I'm connected at a very minor level, for instance, to the rocks lining that firepit," he said as he pointed to the rocks. "But I'm much more closely connected to you two," he said, looking at Esme and Paul, "because we have more in common than I have with a rock. I'm beginning to think that it is this connection, these vibrations, that make telepathy possible."

Wilhelmina spoke for the first time in this discussion. *I wonder if that's why I was able to help Paul learn to speak telepathically with me.*

Sapphire said, *I think so. At first, we dragons thought that only a very few humans had the magic necessary for telepathic communications. But your efforts with Paul caused us to rethink things. There certainly is magic that only some can use. Of that there is no doubt. But I also understand what Tobias was saying. We are all interconnected, and as we each in turn realize our connections with the other life in the world, those connections strengthen.*

Ty nodded. "Tobias also analyzed a lot of children's fairy tales, and he came to some conclusions that frankly have really shaken me. I know I haven't absorbed them fully, but the main points are that our emotions have a lot to do with how we perceive the world. Aloysius thinks that The Wraith is growing in strength because it's feeding off our fears as well as our hatreds.

"We still aren't sure what exactly The Wraith is, but I'm beginning to think that it's some sort of spirit that is gaining a body as it builds strength.

As far as defeating it, the evidence, from Tobias and from the analysis of the ancient legends, is that it can't be defeated by force."

Esme looked fearful. "Then how are we going to beat it? Or will it win?"

Ty said, "I suspect you didn't have anyone read bedtime stories to you, but if you had, you'd have heard that love, joy, harmony, and other positive feelings can drive the darkness away. I think we have to find a way to make Dragonwind the happiest, most loving place on the planet and then trap The Wraith with kindness. It apparently was buried deep within the mines, and Dragonwind is now the nearest village to that spot. I don't know exactly how we're going to do this, but I do know that we need to strengthen Dragonwind into a community where everyone is valued."

Esme looked worried. "I felt the evil when it came that night. It's real. It's terrifying. I don't know how anyone would stand up to it. I know I can't."

Rupert rubbed his head against her leg. *I'll help you.*

Sapphire said very gently, *Ty is correct. Violence will not help and neither will running away or hiding. Esme, you have very powerful and special gifts. We will work with you to strengthen those, and we will help you to learn to handle your fears. You and Paul are important to us all.*

In addition, Ty, while we work with Esme and Paul, you need to help the villagers to strengthen themselves, to unite the new refugees with the current residents, to make a unified whole. I suspect that Drake and his friends won't be giving you anymore trouble, but they should be watched. I think they're too afraid to do anything but hide and save their own skins. It would help if somehow the information of Johnston's demise reached them, with full details that he was frightened to death.

Ty stood. "I can see that the word spreads. Esme, Paul, trust Sapphire, Magnolia, and Wilhelmina. They will guide you and help you learn what you need to know. I'll be checking in with you soon."

Ty leaped onto Criseda, and they took off for Dragonwind. Once they were out of sight, Sapphire said, *Shall we continue our lessons?*

Esme looked apprehensive, but Paul nodded. "Sure."

Wilhelmina nudged Esme with her head. *You're safe with us. We're going to help you to learn that the world is a good place. You've had so much horror in your life that you've learned to believe that the world is a dark and scary place. That belief colors everything you see, everything you do. You tend to forget the good moments, and when the bad moments come, they dominate your view of the world. Nightmares, for instance, become so powerful that you have trouble sleeping. You worry constantly. You're on alert for the next disaster, which you know is coming.*

Our beliefs govern our realities. If we can help you focus on the positive, on the good in this world, then you will be better able to cope when challenges arise, as they surely will, but you won't be constantly looking for disasters. Instead, you'll see the beauty that surrounds you.

Esme thought for a long time and then finally said, in a timid voice, "I'll try."

Magnolia said, *That's all any of us can do.*

CHAPTER 18

VILLAGE CHANGES

When Ty and Criseda arrived at the village green, they were greeted by the sounds of hammers and saws. Ty walked over to the space on the south side of Martha's bakery, where he saw Wilson directing lots of eager helpers. The framing for the new tea shop and community center was taking shape.

"Wow," said Ty. "You've made a lot of progress. Is your own home finished?"

Wilson smiled. "My home is what we call roughed in. It's enough to keep us safe from the winter elements. There is still has a lot of interior work to be done, but I can do that in the winter with help from Selena and probably less help from Ralph. He's only six so not a carpenter yet."

Ty chuckled at that.

Wilson continued. "With winter approaching, I wanted to get as many buildings and homes roughed in as possible. I know that your winters are much like what we had in our old village, and folks won't be comfortable in tents for much longer."

"That is certainly true," said Ty.

"I also wanted to do something for the village after all the kindness everyone has shown to me and my family."

"To be honest, we're lucky to have you," said Ty. "Now how can I help?"

The next few weeks were a buzz of activity in Dragonwind. Everyone seemed determined to get the village community center and tea shop finished. In addition to that building, Wilson had gotten volunteers to work on the remaining homes for the new additions to the village. Ty had allotted land to all who wished to stay. The lands were large enough so that each family could raise food and keep a few goats, cows, or chickens as well.

Everyone seemed excited about all the new additions to Dragonwind, not only the buildings and homes but also the new families. Ty was happy to see how well the new folks were settling in and making friends. The fall weather also proved to be very obliging, allowing the outdoor work, as well as the autumn harvest, to proceed with only occasional delays.

Ty made sure that he took turns working alongside each of the construction crews. He kept an ear out for any difficulties or personality clashes. Further, he planted seeds of information about dealing with The Wraith's henchmen. He realized that most people wouldn't believe him if he tried to explain how thoughts could change reality, but he did think that he could demonstrate how cooperation and talking things through produced better results than angry words or fighting. Only time would tell if his subtle nudges would have any long-term results, but it was all he could think of to do.

Meanwhile, the dragons continued teaching Esme and Paul. Ty knew that they would need to return to Dragonwind before winter, but he wanted to give them as much time with the dragons as the weather permitted. He checked on the two of them many times, and he was pleased that Esme hadn't had a nightmare since she'd started living with the dragons.

Jeb was working on the constructions, but he also stopped by Drake's home fairly frequently, and Miranda and Mirabella kept watch when he wasn't there. Drake and his two friends did not seem at all inclined to move. Ty wasn't surprised but was glad that they were under surveillance.

Everything changed about a month after Esme and Paul went to live with the dragons. Once again, Esme had a horrible nightmare, screaming that her father was coming. But this time, Sapphire, Magnolia, and Wilhelmina made a telepathic shield. Then Sapphire said, *You're safe. Focus your energy on your breathing, the way we practiced.*

Esme said, *I can't. They're going to get me.*

Sapphire and the others sent calming thoughts to Esme as Rupert and Samantha snuggled up close to her. Then Sapphire said, softly and gently, *You can do this. We're right here with you. Breathe slowly and calmly.*

Esme became noticeably calmer.

That's good, said Sapphire. *Now, without any fear, can you tell me what your father is doing? Remember, he can't get to you.*

Esme nodded. *They're coming up the path to Dragonwind. My father and a bunch of men.*

That's good, said Sapphire. *How close to Dragonwind are they? Can you tell?*

They're nearly inside the village.

Sapphire said, *Stay calm. Breathe. We're going to practice the defense I told you about. Ready?*

Ready, said Esme, although there was a hesitation in her thought.

Sapphire turned to Wilhelmina. *Can you alert Ty? He needs to gather any villagers whom he's confident can stand in front of these men and show neither fear nor anger.*

Will do, said Wilhelmina.

Once Wilhelmina had contacted Ty, Sapphire said, *Now, Esme, you're going to use your special gift, your ability to read minds. Can you look into your father's mind?*

Esme clung tightly to Rupert. *He's going to try to set fire to the village.*

Sapphire said, *That's good, Esme.*

No, it's not good, said Esme, beginning to panic. *They'll hurt people.*

Sapphire sent more calming thoughts to Esme. *It's good that we know what he wants to do. Wilhelmina is warning Ty. What you need to do is send thoughts to your father the way I taught you. You need to sneak into his head and gently nudge his thoughts toward leaving the village. You need to let him know that no one here will hurt him and that no one here is afraid of him. Can you do that?*

I'll try, said Esme.

As Esme was doing that, Wilhelmina was talking to Ty. *Have they arrived yet?*

Ty answered, *They're just walking into the village—or maybe I should say swaggering into the village. They look pretty confident. I have at least half the villagers standing with me.*

Wilhelmina said, *Just stay smiling and nonconfrontational and let me know what's going on. Esme is trying to get into her father's head.*

Ty answered, *Will do. Right now her father is demanding that I hand her over. I've explained that she isn't here. Hold on. He's looks confused. He's shaking his head. Now he's looking scared. He just yelled, "Get out of my head. I don't know you." He's banging a fist against his head. He's stomping and twisting around.*

Wilhelmina smiled. *Maybe Esme has reached him.*

Ty said, *Now he's shouting, "I need to get my daughter. I know she's here. I'll be killed if I don't get her." His men are looking at him as if they think he's lost his mind. Now they seem scared. You won't believe it. They're leaving. He's saying, "This is some trick. Don't think you've gotten away with it. I will be back." But for now, they're leaving. Way to go, Esme. I'll be eager to hear what she did, but we're all good now.*

Nice job, Ty. Talk with you tomorrow, said Wilhelmina.

Sapphire spoke to Esme. *Now just watch your father and be sure his intentions are to leave. Once you're sure he's going to go back, you can gently tell him what a good job he did and then withdraw from his mind.*

Esme followed Sapphire's instructions to the letter. Once she pulled out of her father's mind, she sagged down on her bed. Rupert and Samantha sat right next to her. Finally, Esme said, *That was scary. And hard.*

Sapphire said, *I know. But you were never in any danger. Magnolia, Wilhelmina, and I kept you shielded and safe. You just needed to trust us. And trust yourself. You did all the work.*

Wish I'd known how to do that years ago, said Esme. *I could have really hurt him.*

No! said Sapphire firmly. *You never, ever use your gift to hurt anyone. That would severely damage you. Furthermore, it wouldn't work. Your father knows how to deal with attacks. He doesn't know what to do with kindness. The whole point of the interconnectivity of all things is to bring us closer, not rip us apart. And if your father had been close to The Wraith, I'm pretty sure what you did today wouldn't have worked. We were very lucky tonight. We'll need to do more in the future, but the main thing is that you can't be hurt. You don't need to be afraid.*

Esme thought for a few minutes. *I think I get it. But you'll help me if he comes back, won't you?*

Yes, I will. Now go back to sleep, and we'll talk more in the morning.

The next morning, Ty discovered that the villagers had lots of questions. They had done what Ty had asked. They'd stood on the village green in front of the men who were threatening their village, and they'd stayed calm, but they couldn't figure out why the men just left. They were especially confused that the men themselves looked scared and that their leader was acting strangely.

Ty said, "I don't know that I have any answers. What I do know is that if we'd tried to fight them or defend ourselves, our village would have been burned, and we would have been hurt. The threat to our world—and it's bigger than just a threat to Dragonwind, as bad as that would be for us personally—is a battle between good and evil. The evil grows stronger when it's met with either fear or anger. We can't fight it. But we can defeat it. And we will defeat it. We'll defeat it by being unafraid, by not allowing threats to intimidate us, by staying true to ourselves."

"But how can that be?" asked Wilson.

"I'm not entirely sure," said Ty. "But you saw what happened last night. What we need to do now is stay focused on the positives in our village. We need to support one another. United we are strong, if we work together. And look what that has accomplished. Quite aside from confusing the men last night and causing them to leave, look around our village. We have new homes. We have new villagers to fill those homes. We are nearly finished with the Dragonwind tea shop and community center. Together we are unstoppable."

"We have done a lot," said Jeb, nodding in agreement.

"And we'll do more," said Ty. "We'll do it for us, for each and every one of us. And when one of us has a problem, we'll help to solve it. If someone's sick or hurt, we'll pull together to support them. We are a village, and we will stand together."

This brought a rousing cheer from the assembled villagers. Wilson said, "I'm so glad we ended up here. This is a wonderful village."

The meeting broke up then as everyone got back to work. Ty went to talk with Martha.

"Martha, what do you think? Will we really defeat The Wraith?"

Martha looked thoughtful. "The dragons seem to think we can, and I'm holding on to that."

"I guess that's all we can do," Ty said. "If nothing else, the villagers are really pulling together, and that counts for a lot, in my book."

"Mine too," said Martha.

The next morning, Sapphire contacted Ty and asked him to meet with her to discuss Esme and Paul. Ty joined the meeting that had already started and saw Esme, with Rupert and Samantha, and Paul, with Wilhelmina, Sapphire, and Magnolia.

Sapphire thanked Ty for coming. *Esme passed an enormous test last night. She managed to overcome her very real fears of her father. She trusted in our protection, and she influenced her father. She convinced him that he needed to leave.*

Ty said, *Well, he sure was scared, and he acted very strangely, shouting and ranting. They did leave, but he promised that he would return.*

Sapphire nodded. *He will return. Esme was successful primarily because her father was a long way away from The Wraith. It was easier to turn his thoughts toward leaving. I suspect The Wraith will figure that out. When acting against someone as powerful as Esme, The Wraith is going to need to be really close.*

Esme said, "No! I don't want him close. He's really evil, and that makes me sick. And scared."

Wilhelmina nudged Esme on the shoulder. *Remember one lesson you learned last night. You can trust Sapphire, Magnolia, and me. We will keep you safe.*

Esme looked scared. "I'm trying, really I am. But you haven't felt that evil. It's not just bad, like my dad. It goes right to the very core of my being. And it tries to twist me. It wants to control me too. I don't know how to handle that. All I can think of to do is run, but I know I could never run far enough or fast enough."

Sapphire said, *That instinct to run feeds the evil and makes it stronger. You need to trust us to keep you safe and to focus instead on your breathing. You need to think of something really good, something that makes you very happy. That will protect you even better than we can. The Wraith withers under joy and happiness.*

Esme said, "I don't exactly have a lot of happy memories."

Magnolia said, *Then we need to work on helping you have more of them.*

Paul said, "I think flying with Criseda would be a happy memory for you. I can't wait to tell my mom about how great that was."

Esme smiled. "That was pretty great."

You need lots of happy memories, said Sapphire, *and that's why you and Paul, along with Rupert, Samantha, and Wilhelmina, are going to return to Dragonwind.*

"What?" shouted Esme.

It's time, said Sapphire. *We've taught you a lot here. Now you must practice. You need to set aside time for your breathing exercises, and you need to stay focused. But you also need to be a child and have fun. You need to fill yourself with joy and happiness, and that will happen most easily in Dragonwind.*

"But what happens when my dad returns?" asked Esme.

We can put the protective shield over you no matter where you are, said Sapphire. *You need to trust us to keep you safe. You'll have Wilhelmina with you, and she can reach us as well. Thanks to the training we've given you, you will now be just as safe in Dragonwind as you are here.*

"I'm not sure," said Esme.

I know, said Sapphire. *You have trouble trusting, and that's understandable after all you've been through. But you will be safe, I promise.*

Ty helped Esme and Paul pack up their belongings, and then he set them onto Wilhelmina, who offered to carry them down to Dragonwind. Esme held Rupert, and Paul held Samantha. Ty put their baggage onto Criseda, and they flew down ahead of Wilhelmina and her party.

CHAPTER 19

CHALLENGES

Ty and Criseda landed on the village green, and Ty went to find Martha and Naomi to update them that Esme and Paul would be returning shortly. His good news sent the two women into a flurry of activities. Naomi went home to be sure that she had Paul's room just the way he'd want it. He'd never seen the new home, and she wanted him to be impressed.

Martha did more baking, making a cake for each of them, and then started on dinner preparations. Ty smiled as he realized there was going to be a grand celebration for the returning children, which would give Esme another happy memory.

Wilhelmina and company arrived in the middle of the afternoon, and Naomi was thrilled to see that Paul was walking again. His broken leg was healed. He did have a slight limp, and possibly he always would. The break had been nasty. But he could run and jump and was happy to prove this to his mother. Naomi took him to their new home on the forest's edge, listening to Paul chattering on and on about all he'd seen and done with the dragons. Wilhelmina followed along and later told Ty, *Naomi made the rooms big enough so that I can come into the house. I can even sleep in Paul's bedroom, which I think is the largest room in the house.*

That's wonderful, said Ty. *Enjoy.*

Esme was much quieter. Martha gave her a big hug and took her into the house. Esme looked around a bit apprehensively, as Rupert and Samantha followed her to her room. Martha and Ty gave her some time to settle in before they checked on her.

"How did you like living with the dragons?" Martha asked.

"It was very safe," said Esme. "Wish I could have stayed there."

Martha and Ty exchanged glances before Martha said, "Well, we're sure glad you're back. Want to help me bake bread in the morning? I've missed not only you but also your help."

"I guess," said Esme with a noticeable lack of enthusiasm.

"You don't have to," said Martha. "I just thought you might enjoy it."

Esme was really quiet. Finally, Ty said, "Why don't you tell us what's bothering you."

Tears started to fall from Esme's eyes. "I'm scared."

Martha stood up and went over to hug Esme. "You poor child. Of course you are."

"But Sapphire says I shouldn't be. That I should just trust that they'll keep me safe."

Ty said, "Sapphire said that. I did hear her. But I don't think she ever meant to say that it would be easy to trust. You have no reason to trust any of us. It takes time to build trust, especially when you've been through the trauma that you have."

"I know no one here would hurt me," began Esme.

"I believe that is a true statement," said Ty. "The only ones who might have wanted to harm you are no longer a threat. They're so scared that they aren't leaving their home. Miranda, Mirabella, and Jeb are keeping an eye on them.

"That being said," Ty continued, "knowing that we wouldn't harm you is not the same as trusting us to keep you safe. The Wraith is a powerful force, whatever he or it is. I believe that the dragons are more than equal to protecting you from them, and if you add Wilhelmina into the mix, we should be undefeatable. However, we don't know that for sure, and you've been let down so many times that I understand why you're afraid."

"I keep thinking that I should just be able to tell myself that I'm safe," said Esme.

Martha patted Esme's hand. "It doesn't work like that. The more you beat yourself up for not being able just to trust, the worse you'll feel. It's one thing to know something in your head. It's quite another thing to really believe it and make it yours."

"But Sapphire said…" stuttered Esme.

"I know," said Ty. "And maybe it's different for dragons. But the truth is, she knows that we need you to defeat The Wraith. Your special talents are very powerful. However, that being said, we're going to have to find ways to help you without pushing you or scaring you away."

"How are we going to do that?" asked Esme.

"First, Sapphire said that you needed more happy memories, more joy in your life," said Ty. "So we need to start there. While you and Paul were gone, lots has happened. I'd like to walk you around Dragonwind so that you can see all the changes and get to know our new residents."

"I guess," said Esme.

"Paul and Wilhelmina can come with us," said Ty.

"That would be nice," said Esme. "OK, I'll give it a try."

"Why don't you help Martha with the baking in the morning," said Ty. "You're used to that, after all. Then after lunch we'll go on our tour. That means that you have the rest of today just to relax and be with us."

Esme smiled then. "OK, that's sounding better. I can do that."

"Good," said Martha. "After all, we need time to spoil you."

"And it goes without saying that Rupert and Samantha can come with us as well." said Ty.

"Those two are also welcome in the bakery as long as they stay in the back with us," added Martha.

"Thanks so much for understanding," said Esme.

"Just promise us," said Martha, "that you won't withdraw. If you're worried about something or if something isn't working for you, then you need to talk to us."

"Yeah," said Esme, "I've got it. I'm just not used to having anyone to talk to, to having anyone who cares. Thanks!" With that, she stood up and gave both Martha and Ty big hugs.

The next morning, Martha and Esme headed to the bakery, and Martha was pleased to see that Esme really enjoyed herself, once she got back into her routine. Together they baked the day's breads, cakes, cookies, and donuts.

Ty stopped by just before lunch. "How's it going?"

"Really well," said Esme. "Do you like the cookies I made?" she asked, pointing to a sheet of dragon cookies.

"Wow," said Ty. "They look perfect. I'm sure your dragon friends would be very pleased."

"I saved one with turquoise frosting just for you," Esme said as she handed Ty a cookie.

"Thanks," he said as he took a bite. "Tasty as well. Great job!"

"It was really fun," said Esme. She then added, "A happy memory."

"For sure," said Ty. "Shall we head out for your tour of the village?"

Esme turned to look at Martha. "Do you need me to do anything before I leave with Ty?"

Martha smiled. "No, I'm good, but it sure was wonderful having you back."

Esme hugged Martha and said, "I had a really good time."

Then Esme called to Rupert and Samantha, and the three of them followed Ty out of the bakery.

Ty said, "I thought we'd begin at the tea shop. We can eat lunch there if you like."

The tea shop was right next to the bakery. Esme looked at the new building and said, "Wow! This looks really nice."

"Paul's mom, Naomi, is one of the owners. The other owners are her friends from the mining towns who decided to make their homes here in Dragonwind," said Ty as he opened the door into the tea shop.

Esme followed with Rupert and Samantha. She expected that someone would tell her that Rupert and Samantha had to stay outside, but instead, Naomi, who was running the shop for the afternoon, came over and said, "Great to see you all. We have a special eating area for those who want to bring in their fur friends. Let me escort you there."

Sure enough, there was a side room with tables and chairs, and Esme noticed that Rob was there with his dog. Ty and Esme chose a table, and Rupert and Samantha settled at their feet. Naomi handed them menus. "I'll give you a few moments to decide."

Ty and Esme looked over the menu, and Esme said, "They offer quite a few choices. I bet this place will be really popular."

Ty chose a large cheese-and-pickle sandwich, and Esme went with peanut butter and jam, a favorite of hers. When they were finished, Ty paid Naomi, and they thanked her for a lovely lunch. Then the four of them headed back outside.

Ty took Esme out to the edge of the village, where the newcomers had been allotted lands, and showed her all the new homes, some finished, some still under construction. Paul and Wilhelmina came over to say hi, and Paul proudly showed off his new home.

"We've never had anything this nice before," he said. "And look at my bedroom—Wilhelmina has made a sleeping nest in the corner using blankets and pillows my mom gave her. Isn't it wonderful?"

"It sure is," said Ty. "We just had lunch that your mom prepared for us at the new tea shop."

"Yeah, she showed us that this morning and even mentioned that there was a room where people could eat with their fur friends, but unfortunately, it isn't big enough for Wilhelmina," Paul said.

"They're planning on outdoor seating by spring, when the weather's nice, so you guys could eat there then," said Ty.

"Want to come with us to see the rest of the village? Ty's showing me all of Dragonwind," said Esme.

"Sure," said Paul.

The six of them made quite a group as they toured the area. Ty took them past Jeb's forester's cottage and explained how Jeb took care of the forest and all its inhabitants.

Jeb said, "There's not as much to see now, with winter coming, but in the spring, I can always use helpers to clean up after the winter storms. You'd be most welcome."

Paul said, "That sounds like fun! Wilhelmina would enjoy that I'm sure, wouldn't you?" He patted her back.

Sure would. I've already been roaming in the forest, and Jeb, you keep it well managed.

Ty passed her compliment on to Jeb, since Jeb wasn't telepathic, and his friend blushed at the kind words, saying, "Gee, thanks, Wilhelmina. That means a lot coming from you. I know you understand what a living forest requires."

Wilhelmina rubbed her head on his shoulder, and Jeb looked happy. He said, "We have deer and elk, but you're our first moose. I'm honored to have you."

As Ty and the others turned to leave, they heard shouting coming from the village green, so they went to see what was going on. Jeb came as well. As they approached the green, they could see several villagers circled around a group of children. Ty said, "Jeb, can you and Wilhelmina stay with Esme, Paul, Rupert, and Samantha while I figure out what's going on?"

"Sure thing," said Jeb. Ty walked over to the gathering.

Kyle was trying to sort things out when he saw Ty. He breathed a sigh of relief and said, "Ty, thank heavens you're here. These children just arrived here, and as you can see, they're in need of help, but not everyone is thrilled to see them."

One of the village men, George, said, "We can't take in orphan children. We've already had enough new folks."

Ty held up a hand for silence and turned to the children, who seemed to be eight to maybe twelve years old. There were five boys and six girls. None of them had shoes. Their clothing was ragged and thin. They had to be very cold. They were dirty and obviously starving.

"Where are you from?" asked Ty.

Several of the children started talking at the same time, and Ty interrupted. "Just one of you explain, please."

The tallest boy said, "My name is Thomas. We've come from the capital, where we'd been forced to work on a ranch for a rich guy named Lord Gofrond. We're all orphans, and he said he'd bought us and we had to work for him."

"Go on," said Ty.

"We heard from some people who'd fled from Lord Upworth's mines that slavery isn't allowed in Estrea and that if we came to Dragonwind, we'd find nice people who would help us. We've walked all the way from the capital, but now these people say we have to go back."

Ty looked first at the sad, tired, footsore children and then back at his own villagers. He noticed that at least a few of the villagers looked ashamed as they heard Thomas's account.

Finally, Ty said, "Everyone is welcome in Dragonwind."

"But…" spluttered George, but he stopped talking as Ty glared at him.

"I don't know what you're worried about, George. We've been working harmoniously with the recent arrivals, and the village has seen major improvements that have benefitted all of us. So what's the problem now?"

"Well, they're just kids," began George, and Ty noticed that several of the others nodded in agreement. "And look at them, they're dirty and unkempt."

Ty tried to keep the anger from his voice, but his displeasure was evident as he said, "Could you walk here from the capital? Without proper clothing? Without shoes? And if you managed it, don't you think you might be dirty and tired, not to mention very hungry? These are children. How dare you turn on them?"

"Well, where are their parents?" said George, who wasn't going to be talked down easily. "These kids aren't our responsibility."

"Did you listen to Thomas? They're orphans who were sold into slavery. They're victims of the evil that is spreading across our nation, and if we don't stand together, if we can't understand that we're here to help one another, then the evil will win," said Ty.

"So we have to take in everyone, no matter what?" said George. "How will we manage that?"

"Yes, we take in everyone who needs us, and we'll find a way, working together, to manage," said Ty. "The evil force, The Wraith, has a much stronger grip on the capital, so it's only natural that people are looking for safer places. Dragonwind is just one outlying village, but others will also receive requests for help. I can't speak for any other villages, but as long as I'm in charge of Dragonwind, we will be a bastion for compassion. We will open our village and our hearts to one and all. If that doesn't suit you, well, you can always leave, but I really hope, once your initial reaction has passed, that you'll realize the importance of standing together for what is right."

While Ty had been talking, Kyle had gone for Martha, and she bustled over to Ty now. "Can I help?" she asked as she looked at the children.

"Yes, thanks," said Ty. "Can you find some helpers to take these children to be bathed, have their wounds treated, especially their feet, and find some hot food for them?"

"Of course," said Martha.

Ty turned to Thomas. "Please, will you go with Martha here? She'll help you all."

Thomas nodded and Ty said, "Martha, this is Thomas. I'm sure he'll assist you."

Martha shook Thomas's hand. "Glad to meet you. Now if you and your friends will come with me, we'll see about helping you."

As the group moved off, George said, "I really don't know about this, but you have always steered us in the right direction. I hope you know what you're doing now."

"Thanks, George," said Ty, holding out his hand to the man, who shook it. "These are difficult times, but in such times, we must always stand for what's right and good."

With that, the group of villagers dispersed. Jeb came up to Ty and said, "Esme's worried. She needs to talk with you."

Ty looked around to be sure no one was in earshot. "What's up, Esme?"

"These kids have been slaves, and they have walked from the capital, but there's one boy in the mix, someone named Bruce, who's not what he seems. He's been fooling the others. He has food in his pockets, and he's gotten help from one of The Wraith's henchmen along the way. He insisted they come all the way to Dragonwind, even though there were closer villages whose people offered to help them," said Esme.

"Let's go find him and see what he has to say," said Ty.

Martha had taken all the children to the new community center, and she was just starting to assign them to villagers to help them. Ty walked up to Thomas and said, "Which one is Bruce?"

Thomas pointed to another boy, and Ty went over to him. Jeb and Esme stayed in the background, Esme holding Samantha and Rupert right next to her.

Ty walked up to the boy Thomas had indicated and said, "Are you Bruce?"

"Yeah," said the boy. "Why?"

"Would you please empty your pockets?" asked Ty as he noticed that Bruce's clothes were nowhere near as thin and ragged as everyone else's and that his feet didn't look as injured.

"Why should I?" asked Bruce.

"Because I said so," said Ty. "Either empty them or we'll empty them for you."

With reluctance, but faced with Ty's determined look, Bruce emptied his pockets. Thomas and the others watched, and their mouths dropped as they saw the bread rolls and meat that Bruce pulled from his pockets.

Thomas shouted, "Where did you get all that food?"

Bruce sneered, "Wouldn't you like to know? You're all fools."

Ty grabbed Bruce, twisted his right arm behind him, and said, "Who are you working for?"

"Wouldn't you like to know?" said Bruce.

Esme stepped forward. "He's working for Lord Gofrond, who's working for The Wraith."

"How…" stuttered Bruce, "do you know that?"

"Easy," said Esme, "I just read your mind."

"Thanks, Esme," said Ty. Then he turned to Bruce. "Do you deny it?"

"No," said Bruce, "but if they find out that you know, they'll kill me."

"Maybe you should have thought of that before you agreed to help them," said Ty.

"I didn't have a choice," said Bruce.

"You had a choice about sharing your food with the others," said Ty. "And your feet aren't all that injured. You've had help on the journey that you didn't share with the others. Were you even a slave?"

"I can't tell you," said Bruce, now looking scared.

"He's the son of Lord Gofrond's foreman," said Esme. "He's just pretending to be an orphan."

"They can't know that you figured that out," said Bruce, panic rising in his voice. "They'll kill me."

"That's not our problem," said Ty. "Out on the village green, I said we'd help anyone who needed it, but you don't qualify for that."

"What are you going to do with me?" asked Bruce.

"What were you supposed to do once you got here?" asked Ty. "Why didn't you stop at any of the other villages where help was offered to you?"

"They told me we had to get to Dragonwind," said Bruce, "and then I was to make friends with her," he continued as he pointed to Esme, "and get her outside the village so they could take her."

"They sent a boy because they were too afraid to do it themselves," said Ty. "Cowards."

"What are you going to do to me?" asked Bruce.

"You're going back home," said Ty. "My dragon will fly you to Lord Gofrond's lands and drop you off."

"You can't," cried Bruce. "They'll kill me."

Ty thought for a few minutes. "If you're truly afraid for your life, then you may stay here and work off your punishment by helping the village."

"You can't make me," snapped Bruce.

"Listen, son," said Ty in a kinder voice. "Each of us is responsible for our actions. I understand that you did things because you were afraid. However, you're safe now. And you could have helped the others or warned us when you arrived, but you did neither. You have a lot to answer for, and I'm giving you a safe way to work off your debt."

"I don't owe anyone anything," said Bruce. "My dad is a really important man."

Ty said, "You can't have it both ways. If you fear for your life, then your dad can't be that important. This is your choice to make. You can either be taken back to your dad, or you can work for us. Which is it to be?"

Bruce was quiet for a few minutes. "I guess I'll work."

Esme spoke up. "Ty, he's saying that because he thinks there will be a way to get me out of the village if he stays here."

"You witch," snarled Bruce.

Esme went on. "He is convinced that he can still complete the job he was given. He sees nothing wrong with what he's done. He thinks that the other children are worthless and that everyone here is weak for trying to help."

Ty said, "Thanks, Esme." Then he turned to Bruce. "Is what she said true?"

"So what?" said Bruce. "My dad and those who work for The Wraith have all the power. The Wraith is going to take over this world, and we'll then be the ones with power. You all are fools if you think you can defeat him."

"I guess you've made your decision then. We'll return you to your father." Bruce said, "But not until I get her." He pointed at Esme.

"You don't get it, do you?" said Ty. "Esme is staying here and she's going to be safe with us."

"They'll kill me if I come back without her," yelled Bruce.

"So you keep saying," said Ty. "You should have thought of that before you did what you did. Once again, I remind you that if you'd shared your food, if you'd warned us as soon as you arrived, if you were truly sorry for your actions, then we would have helped you. But you did nothing, and you're still trying to kidnap Esme. You're still working for The Wraith. I'm sorry, son, but every action has consequences."

"You're all just a bunch of losers," said Bruce. "The Wraith can't be defeated. OK, send me back. I've learned a lot about this village and I'll tell everyone just how weak you really are. I'll be on the winning side. You'll see."

Ty shook his head as he escorted Bruce out to the village green. Then he called to Criseda. *I have someone who needs to be delivered to Lord Gofrond's estate. Will you take him? I don't want him left on his own.*

Sure thing, said Criseda.

She arrived five minutes later and picked Bruce up using her left front claw. He dangled below her as she took off. *He's not going to have a very comfortable trip, but it sounds as if he doesn't deserve one.*

Thanks, Criseda, said Ty, and he went back into the village hall. Martha had found women to assist her, and they were busy helping the other children. Ty checked on the others and learned that they were exactly what they'd claimed. Thomas said, "I wasn't really sure about Bruce. Honestly, I had no idea what he was up to. I knew he hadn't worked with us, but I thought he was just from another slave gang. Lord Gofrond has many of them. I can't believe he kept food and didn't share it. We're starving."

"I'm sorry," said Ty, "and I'm sorry for all you've been through and that you had to walk such a distance. But we'll take care of you and help you find a better place."

Several village men had brought in large tubs filled with hot water. They used sheets hung from the rafters to divide the room into a boys' side and a girls' side, and soon all the orphans were bathing. Once Martha deemed that they were truly clean, they were given fresh clothing, borrowed from villagers who had children of the same size, and then they sat at a long trestle table in the room to eat a nourishing vegetable stew with fresh bread.

By the time everyone had been fed, the children were looking much better. Martha had to bandage all their feet. "It will take a while before their cuts heal, but I'll make sure to check them every day for any signs of infection."

Ty asked the villagers for volunteers to take the children into their homes. They discovered that among the four boys and six girls, there were some siblings. There was a brother/sister pair and a sister/sister pair. Ty made sure that the siblings were kept together. Naomi offered to take one of the boys, and several others among the new arrivals offered their homes. Soon all ten children were being taken to their new lodgings.

By the time all the orphans were settled, Criseda had returned. *I flew over Lord Gofrond's mansion, swooping down low enough so that I could release Bruce on the front driveway. He rolled a bit and probably was shaken, but he wasn't injured. I saw men running out of the mansion as I flew off. So they know that Bruce failed. And they'll soon know something of Esme's powers.*

Thanks, Criseda, said Ty. *I don't think Esme's powers will come as a surprise, but we'll have to stay extra vigilant to keep her safe.*

Criseda nodded and then took off for home.

Ty walked over to Jeb, Esme, Rupert, and Samantha. "I'm so proud of you, Esme," he said. "That took real courage to speak up. It was one thing to tell me about Bruce, but you didn't have to speak in front of him to make sure we knew the truth."

"I was so mad at him," said Esme. "Did you see Thomas and the others? It's a four-hour horse ride to get here from the capital. You've told me that. I can't even imagine how long they've been walking. And with no shoes, no proper clothes, no food? That's real courage. I'm sorry that Bruce didn't let them get help in other villages that were closer, but personally, I'm proud to call them fellow villagers. That was an amazing trek. I couldn't let Bruce get away with lies after all he put them through."

Ty gave her a hug. "You truly are amazing. Let's call it a day now. I'm sure Martha has saved some dinner for us."

CHAPTER 20

REPERCUSSIONS

Ty tossed and turned all night and finally decided that he needed to talk with King Bertram. He also wanted Esme to come with him. He thought he'd need her skills, and he wanted the king to meet her properly, now that she was healed. He knew it would be hard for her to go back to the capital, so he'd tried to figure out another plan. She'd been through so much, but he couldn't think of any other way to learn more.

First thing in the morning, after he'd fed Foxy, he and Criseda headed to Martha's. He found Martha and Esme, along with Rupert and Samantha, in the bakery making the last of the day's baked goods.

"Morning, Ty," said Esme.

"Can we get you something?" asked Martha.

"Sure," said Ty. "A breakfast roll and tea would be nice. Then I need to talk with you both."

Esme got the breakfast roll while Martha made the tea. Ty took a bite of the roll and sipped the tea. "I'm going to see King Bertram. I need to talk to him about this trafficking in orphan children."

"It's horrible to think that something like that is going on," said Martha.

"It certainly is," said Ty. Then he turned to Esme. "I hate to ask you, but I need you to come with me."

Esme turned white. "To the capital? Where my parents are?"

"Yes," said Ty, "but we'll be in the palace. They won't know you're there. And Rupert and Samantha can come with us as well. I know I'm asking a lot, but we need your gifts to get to the bottom of this."

Esme looked down at her hands and was very quiet for several minutes. "Do I have to go? Am I being used by you the way I was used by my parents?"

"No," said Ty. "You are free to say no, if that's what your heart tells you to do. Unlike your parents, I see you as a real person, a wonderful, generous, loving person who's been through an incredibly horrible time. However, if it weren't for your magic, I wouldn't be asking you, so in a way, yes, I'm also in need of your talent. But I'm asking you in order to stop all this, to find out who's behind the child trafficking, who's trying to destroy Estrea. I believe that's a lot different from what your parents were doing."

"I know," said Esme, as tears stole down her cheeks. "But it's really scary."

Martha held her tight. "Ty wouldn't have asked if he could have found any other way to sort out this mess. And he will keep you safe. You'll be with him and Criseda, in addition to Rupert and Samantha. King Bertram is really nice. He has five children of his own and is a very caring man. He'll keep you safe as well."

"The sooner we put a stop to all that's going on, the sooner you won't have to fear being kidnapped or hurt," said Ty.

Esme reached for her handkerchief and dried her tears before answering. "OK, I'll go with you if you really think it will help."

Martha insisted on packing them a bundle of food, even though Ty assured her that they'd be fed at the palace. "You never know when you might get hungry," said Martha.

Out on the village green, Ty lifted Esme onto Criseda's back, then handed Samantha and Rupert up to her. He tied Martha's food onto Criseda before he vaulted up in front of Esme. "Hold on to me," said Ty "and keep Rupert and Samantha between us."

Soon they were in the air, flying to the palace.

They landed in the palace courtyard about an hour later, and Ty helped Esme and her friends down. Esme stared around her in awe. She'd never seen such magnificence. Ty led her up to the palace entrance and let her pull the bell cord.

Henry answered the door. "Hi, Henry. This is Esme, Rupert, and Samantha," Ty said, as Henry led them into the palace.

"Pleased to meet you, Esme, and you, Samantha. Rupert, good to see you again. You've been missed."

"Is the king free?" asked Ty. "We really need to see him."

"I believe so," said Henry. "Let me take you to his office."

Henry led them down a long corridor and then turned into another and finally one more long hallway, where eventually they reached a closed door. Henry knocked and then opened the door. "Ty, Esme, Rupert, and Samantha to see you, sir."

Bertram stood and walked around his desk to greet them. "Hi, Ty. I see you've brought me more company. Rupert, I have missed our chats, but I understand you've been helping Esme. That's very important work. Esme, I hardly recognized you. You look so much better than the night we met in the palace garden," he said as he held out his hand, which Esme shook a bit apprehensively. Finally, the king said, "And you're Samantha. I don't believe I've ever had a squirrel in my office, but I'm certainly glad to have you here. I know you've also been a big help to Esme."

Samantha dipped her head and then moved closer to Esme.

King Bertram said, "Now, come, sit down. Make yourselves comfortable. Henry, can you bring us some tea and sandwiches?"

"Certainly, Sire," said Henry, and he turned and left the room.

"What brings you here this morning?" said King Bertram. "It must be important if you were willing to return to the capital, Esme. I don't imagine you have any good memories from here."

Ty said, "I think Wilhelmina will have told you about the latest arrivals in Dragonwind."

"She has, and I must say I'm horrified to find out that there are those who are selling and enslaving children. Wilhelmina described their journey, and I'm just amazed that they made it to you. I'm glad they're now safe, but we need to put an end to this immediately."

"That's why we're here," said Ty. "Bruce, the boy who was not a slave and who was supposed to capture Esme, said his father is Lord Gofrond's foreman. Have you had any luck investigating Lord Gofrond?"

"Not much," said King Bertram. "As soon as word got out about Lord Upworth's actions and what happened to him, Lord Gofrond tendered his resignation from my advisory committee and withdrew from the capital to his estates. I tried sending some of my men there to question him, but he refused to talk to them."

"Well, now we have some evidence," said Ty. "I think he has to be confronted."

"I agree," said King Bertram. "And I think I should accompany you."

"It could be dangerous," said Ty.

King Bertram looked at Esme. "If this young lady is going, then so am I. We'll take Foster and Oscar. I can ride whichever one of them is willing to take me, and maybe we'll also take Simion, the captain of my guards, if the dragons are willing."

They all walked back out to the courtyard. King Bertram walked over to Foster and Oscar. *Would you two be willing to transport me and Simion to Lord Gofrond's. Ty, Criseda, and his friends will be going as well.*

Foster bowed his head. *It would be our honor.*

King Bertram called to Simion, who was on the palace ramparts inspecting his men. "Simion, we're going for a ride. I want you to send a platoon of guards to Lord Gofrond's estates as quickly as possible."

If Simion was surprised by this order, he gave no sign of it. He merely saluted and then ran down the stairs into the courtyard. He issued orders to his second-in-command to ride immediately and at speed to Lord Gofrond's estates. Then he turned to the king for further instructions.

It was decided that the king would ride on Foster, and Simion would ride Oscar. Both dragons bent their left front legs to make a step, and Ty showed the king and Simion how to get onto their dragons, where to hold on, and a bit about what to expect.

Then Ty got Esme, Rupert, and Samantha onto Criseda before he himself vaulted up. They all took off for Lord Gofrond's estates. It took about a half hour to reach them, and the dragons landed in front of Lord Gofrond's mansion.

Once they all dismounted, Simion pulled the bell cord on the front door. A harried-looking butler answered.

Simion said, "The king would like to see Lord Gofrond."

"I'm so-o-orry," stammered the butler, "but he's not here."

Esme turned to the king and Ty and said, loudly enough for the butler to hear, "Yes he is. He's in his office."

The butler then said, "He's not seeing anyone. He asked not to be disturbed."

The king stepped forward. "He'll see me if he knows what's good for him. Take us to him."

"I-I-I can't," said the butler.

"Fine, then," said the king. "We'll just find him on our own."

The king brushed past the butler, who then apparently decided that he shouldn't let the king roam the mansion on his own. The butler scurried ahead of the king and said, "This way, Your Majesty."

Simion, Ty, Esme, and her friends followed closely behind the king. It didn't take long to reach Lord Gofrond's office. The butler knocked and opened the door but didn't have the courage to announce the guests. He just turned tail and left as quickly as he could.

"What's the meaning of this?" said Lord Gofrond.

"You dare ask," said the king, "with what you're doing?"

"I have no idea what you're talking about," said Lord Gofrond, "and I don't appreciate your showing up unannounced."

"I'm talking about the slaves you have, children, that you have bought from child traffickers and are keeping here to work your lands," said the king. "I knew you were ambitious and greedy, but I never would have thought you would stoop so low."

"You have no proof," said Lord Gofrond.

"Yes, actually we do," said Ty. "Didn't your foreman's son, Bruce, tell you what happened in Dragonwind yesterday?"

"He's been severely punished," said Lord Gofrond. "He acted by himself."

"Then who supplied him with food along their lengthy march?" said Ty. "You were behind this."

"You can't prove anything," said Lord Gofrond.

Esme tugged on Ty's shirt. "He has papers in his left-hand desk drawer that detail all his slave-buying transactions. He's been buying them from someone named Lord Plumfield."

Simion stepped around to the side of Lord Gofrond's desk and pulled out the drawer Esme had mentioned. He took out all the files and handed them to the king.

The king started flipping through the files, handing some to Ty. Lord Gofrond tried to deny that he knew anything, but he turned silent after one glare from the king.

Finally the king said, "These records clearly show that you've been buying children as slaves for the last ten years."

"They're just orphans," said Lord Gofrond. "No one wants them."

"The fact that they're alone in the world should have made you more compassionate, not less," said the king.

"The children who arrived in Dragonwind yesterday," said Ty, "were starving. They had no shoes. Their clothes were little more than rags."

"So?" said Lord Gofrond. "I wasn't responsible for them. My foreman saw to everything."

"Don't give me that nonsense," said the king. "You're his boss. It's your responsibility to know how your lands are run. Well, they won't be your lands anymore."

The king turned to Simion. "How long before your men arrive?"

"They should be here any minute," said Simion. "I'll go outside and wait for them. What are your orders?"

"I want you to round up any of Lord Gofrond's employees, and I want you to hunt for more children," said the king.

"Yes, Sire," said Simion as he left the room.

"You won't get away with this," said Lord Gofrond. "You won't even know what hit you after Lord Plumfield is done with you."

"We just finished a war with his nation," said King Bertram. "They won't be eager to start another."

Esme tugged on the king's arm. He bent down and she whispered, "Lord Plumfield is a puppet for The Wraith. Lord Gofrond is terrified of both of them."

The king nodded and then whispered back, "How does Lord Gofrond communicate with them?"

Esme was quiet for a few minutes. "He gets orders in his head. I think that means that either Lord Plumfield or The Wraith communicates telepathically. Lord Gofrond can't contact them. He has to wait for them to contact him. He can't answer back. He can only receive orders. Every few weeks, Lord Plumfield comes here to talk directly to Lord Gofrond and to collect his money. Lord Gofrond has to pay a lot to Lord Plumfield to keep his lands, and that's why Lord Gofrond worked with Lord Upworth to get money. Those chests Ty found must belong to Lord Gofrond."

"Thanks, Esme," said the king. He turned back to Lord Gofrond. "It seems you're in a lot of trouble. Apparently you won't be able to pay Lord Plumfield what you owe him when he comes next. And you have no way to contact him. You can only receive orders from him."

Lord Gofrond said, "They've promised to take you down."

"How interested do you think they'll be in doing that now that you and Lord Upworth have been exposed? And now that they've lost six chests of gold and silver," said the king.

Lord Gofrond turned very pale at this last statement. "You can't have found the chests. They were hidden."

Ty said, "Yeah, they were hidden by children in dangerous mine shafts, and most of those children were killed. However, we found out about the chests, and right now, they're in a very safe place where you'll never find them. I suspect your greedy masters will not be pleased at how you and Lord Upworth have failed so horribly."

Simion came back into the room. "We found over fifty children in very poor shape. The foreman and his underlings are spilling everything they know, hoping it will save them. They say they only followed Lord Gofrond's orders."

"Lies," said Lord Gofrond, but there wasn't a lot of conviction in his voice.

"Did you find out when Lord Plumfield is expected back?" asked the king.

"He's supposed to arrive one week from today," said Simion.

King Bertram thought for several minutes. "Simion, see if there are any wagons, enough to take all the children back to the palace. They must be our first priority. Then if you have enough transport, I'd like you to arrest the foreman and anyone else who you think is part of this slavery/trafficking ring."

"Yes, Sire," said Simion, and he left to follow his orders.

"Ty, you and I will stay here, along with Esme, Rupert, Samantha, and the three dragons. And Lord Goforth. We will go through this place with a fine-toothed comb, looking at all his records, figuring out how widespread this conspiracy is. I need to know if anyone else other than Lord Goforth and Lord Upworth are involved."

"You have no right to do that," said Lord Goforth.

"We have every right," said the king. "You have not only broken several laws but also have broken every possible code of conduct for human decency. You now have no rights. Soon you will have no money, no property, no titles. If you're very cooperative, you might have your life spared, but don't think you're getting anything else."

The king looked at Esme, and he smiled kindly at her. "You've been a lot of help already. For that I thank you. If you discover anything else, just let us know. I suspect you'll be able to tell us where to look, as Lord Gofrond will try to hide any information."

"Well," said Esme as a grin spread across her face, "he does have a safe in the basement, hidden behind his wine barrels."

Lord Gofrond spluttered and said, "She's a witch."

"Think what you like," said the king. "Esme has suffered at the hands of your master more than just about anyone. She has every right to see his empire collapse. Ty, secure this miserable piece of humanity so that he can't escape, and let's get searching."

They found a large safe just where Esme had said it would be. Esme then added, "The combination is 4-82-9."

"Thanks, Esme," said the king as Ty dialed the combination. Inside the safe they found quite a bit of gold and silver. They also found records for the estate going back more than forty years.

King Bertram looked around the basement and finally found some empty wooden crates. "Let's load all this into crates and then I think this needs to get somewhere much safer right away. Any suggestions?"

"Oscar could fly it to the palace if you want, or if you don't think that's safe enough, I'm sure Sapphire would keep the crates," said Ty.

"Since we keep being told that there's a strong possibility of danger to me and the palace, let's have Oscar take them to Sapphire," said the king.

Ty, Esme, and Bertram filled two wooden crates with the contents of the safe. Ty carried one of them as Bertram carried the other, and they went up the stairs and then out to the front courtyard of the mansion.

Oscar, said Ty, *you keep saying you're bored. How'd you like to fly these valuable crates to Sapphire for safekeeping? We need to get them there as soon as possible.*

Oscar practically swelled with pride at the mission. *I'll get them there right away. You can count on me.*

Thanks, Oscar, said Ty as he secured the crates onto Oscar's sides. *And then hurry back. We need all the help we can get.*

Sure thing, said the proud orange dragon, and he took off immediately.

Young whelp, said Foster with a note of indulgence in his thoughts. *But he'll do a good job, and he won't stop until he has those crates safely hidden.*

I know, said Ty. *But I'll be glad when he's back. We may have a week, but on the other hand, there are no guarantees of that.*

Simion came up to the king, saluted, and said, "We're all loaded up. I have the children, as well as a few household servants who didn't want to stay any longer, in one wagon, and the foreman and his helpers in another, guarded by two of my men."

"Safe travels," said the king. "Please tell Queen Elicia that she has my permission to take care of the children in any way that she finds workable. They will need a lot of attention, I know. And thank her for me. Let her know I'll be home once this is settled, in a week or so."

"Yes, sir," said Simion. He saluted and left the courtyard.

The king watched him go. "I wish we had a telepath at the palace now so that we could have alerted Elicia and so that we'd know when Simion arrived. Maybe when this is all over, you could look into finding someone."

Rupert said, *I'm sorry I've deserted you, King. But Esme's need seemed much greater.*

The king bent to pat Rupert's head. *I agree, and I'm glad Esme has you. I didn't mean any criticism of you at all. It just seems as if we need more human telepaths. We thought we just had two of us, Ty and me, and now we also have Esme and Paul. But that's still not enough. Let's keep searching, and we'll worry about telepaths later on.*

They searched all of Lord Gofrond's estate, and although they found more evidence of the horrible living conditions that the children had been kept in, they didn't find any other hidden treasures or records. Esme was able to find two more nobles who profited from the child trafficking by reading Lord Gofrond's mind, and she learned that Lord Plumfield was not acting for his country's government. He was just a greedy, thoroughly nasty human being, and King Bertram hoped that Mlinred's king would punish him once King Bertram informed him of what was going on.

Oscar returned two days after he'd left with the chests. He'd stopped at the palace on his way to Lord Gofrond's estate. Both Sapphire and Foster had apparently suggested that he do that. He reported to King Bertram. *Queen Elicia says that she has things well in hand at the palace. The children are all being cared for. Some needed quite a bit of medical care, and they all were starving, but they are managing much better now, although several of them still suffer from nightmares. The queen asks that you take care of yourself, and she will be happier when you're back home.*

King Bertram smiled. *Thank you, Oscar. And thank you for stopping at the palace. We're glad to have you back here. I suspect we're going to need everyone's help once Lord Plumfield arrives.*

Oscar said, *Simion and his troops are also on their way back here. He should arrive by morning. He said to let you know that the palace is well guarded. He wants to be sure you are also.*

Again, that's good news, said King Bertram. *I suspect the queen had a hand in that, but I also suspect she's right in sending the troops here.*

CHAPTER 21

CONFRONTATIONS

Lord Plumfield arrived two days later, accompanied by six men. King Bertram's guards quickly surrounded them, took away their bows and arrows, and herded them into a small pantry off the kitchen. Lord Plumfield was escorted none too gently into Lord Gofrond's office, where King Bertram, Ty, and Esme were seated, with Rupert and Samantha at Esme's side.

"What's the meaning of this?" demanded Lord Plumfield. "And where's Lord Gofrond?"

"He's being detained, awaiting trial," said King Bertram. "Why are you here?"

"That's none of your business," said Lord Plumfield.

"He's here for his money and to get Lord Gofrond to buy twenty more slave children. The children are on their way here in a wagon and will arrive by nightfall," said Esme.

"What? How do you know that?" said Lord Plumfield.

"Is she correct?" asked King Bertram.

"That's none of your business," repeated Lord Plumfield.

"You're in my lands now, so it is my business," said King Bertram. "It might also interest you to know that we now have all Lord Gofrond's treasures as well as all the former Lord Upworth's. There will be no money for you."

Lord Plumfield blanched on hearing this news. "But I have to have that. You don't know what will happen to me if I don't take the gold and silver back with me."

"Oh, we have a pretty good idea," said Ty, "and frankly, we don't care. Does your king know what you've been doing?"

"Certainly," said Lord Plumfield.

"No," said Esme firmly. "His king has no idea. Lord Plumfield didn't like the peace treaty, and now he's doing his best to bring you down, King Bertram, and start another war. Wars are profitable for him, and he needs money."

"Thanks, Esme," said the king. He turned to Lord Plumfield. "I'll be sure to get word to the king of Mlinred immediately and let him know what you've been up to. I'm sure he'll want to know. He can then decide what to do with you."

Ty said, "The capital of Mlinred is only an hour's flight from here, Your Majesty. If you like, Criseda and I could return him to King Joseph."

"No!" shouted Lord Plumfield.

"What a good idea, Ty," said King Bertram. "Just let me write a note to Joseph explaining all this."

King Bertram picked up a quill, dipped it into an ink bottle, and began writing. After a few minutes, he looked up at Lord Plumfield. "Are any others in Mlinred involved in this plot?"

"No," said Lord Plumfield.

"Yes," said Esme. "There are four other lords involved." She gave King Bertram their names.

"Thank you, Esme," said King Bertram, and he continued writing. When he was done, he signed and sealed the document and handed it to Ty. "Get this piece of scum out of my sight. We'll wait here until the caravan with the children arrives, and then we'll head back to the palace. I let King Joseph know that we'll care for the children, but if he wants them back, he is welcome to send a proper escort for them."

Ty grabbed Lord Plumfield by his left arm and marched him out of the room. As they got to the door, Ty turned. "Criseda and I should be back in a little over two hours."

Outside, Ty asked Criseda if she'd carry Lord Plumfield. Lord Plumfield screamed when she picked him up in her left front claws. Ty vaulted onto her back, and they set off to Mlinred's capital.

Ty was true to his word. He and Criseda arrived back at Lord Gofrond's estate two and a half hours later. He reported to King Bertram. "King Joseph was horrified to hear about what his nobles had been doing, and he promised he'd close down the operation in Mlinred. He stripped Lord Plumfield of his lands and titles and threw him into prison. His wife and four children will have to leave their lands. King Joseph will provide them with a cottage on the palace grounds for now. He also sent guards to arrest the others named in your report to him."

"Excellent," said Bertram. "So the plot has been foiled."

Simion came into the office. "The wagon from Mlinred has arrived, Sire. We've fed the children and given them blankets, but we need to get them proper clothing and a place to stay. I think we're ready to head for the palace."

"Excellent," said King Bertram. "Do you have a way to take Lord Gofrond into custody for transport to the palace, or would it be easier to have one of the dragons carry him?"

Simion smiled. "Oh, if the dragons are willing, I think that would be best."

"Right," said King Bertram, also smiling. "I'm sure Oscar will be most happy to have that detail. You and your men head out with the children, and we'll fly with the dragons as we did when we arrived. Oh, and when you're ready to leave, you may let Lord Plumfield's men out of the pantry. They can make their own way back home, on foot, I think."

"Yes, Sire," said Simion. He saluted and left.

Ty retrieved Lord Gofrond from the room where he'd been locked up. Then he took the prisoner out to the front of the mansion, where he saw that King Bertram had already mounted onto Foster, after lifting Esme, Rupert, and Samantha onto Criseda.

"Aren't you getting to be an accomplished dragon rider?" said Ty with a chuckle.

"I don't think I'd say that, but Foster was very helpful," said King Bertram.

Ty took Lord Gofrond over to Oscar. *Are you willing to take this prisoner?*

Sure, said Oscar, and he grabbed Lord Gofrond in his right front claw, none too gently.

Ty vaulted onto Criseda in front of Esme, and the three dragons took flight.

Later, as they were landing in the palace courtyard, Ty had an urgent call from Wilhelmina. *Ty, we need you and Esme to get back here as quickly as possible. We think an assault is being planned on Dragonwind.*

Ty said, *We've just landed at the palace. We'll take off immediately and head your way.*

Ty saw that King Bertram was talking with his wife. Ty turned to Esme, Rupert, and Samantha. "You three sit tight up here. I'm going to report to the king and then we have to head immediately for Dragonwind."

"What's—" began Esme and then she stopped because she knew what was happening. She just nodded.

Ty went over to the king and queen. "Sir, there's trouble heading toward Dragonwind. We have to go."

"Certainly," said Bertram.

"I think I might know something about that," said the queen. "I was just telling Bertram that we received word that Esme's mother has been killed. The neighbors also said that her father is acting really insane, much more than they've ever seen. His eyes are glowing red, and he's been attacking everyone around him."

"That sure can't be good," said Ty. "OK, thanks for letting me know. I'll update you on what's happening as soon as I can."

Ty vaulted back onto Criseda just as Aloysius came hurrying out of the palace. He shouted, "Wait, Ty. I have more information."

"Can it wait?"

"No, it is really important," said Aloysius as he hurried over to Criseda's side. "I've been looking into more records about evils that don't seem human. I've found something that I think might fit The Wraith. I also have an idea about defeating him if this is what he is."

"That is important," said Ty. "Tell me."

"There have been several references over the centuries to an evil spirit who's able to take over human bodies. Needless to say, there's no common description of this being since the bodies are all different. But the one thing they all have in common is red eyes," said Aloysius.

"So it might have taken over Stephen," said Ty.

"Yes," agreed Aloysius. "This spirit lies dormant for years, even centuries. It has reappeared only a few times that have been recorded, and each time the reappearance has been associated with a mine that has been dug exceptionally deep."

"OK," said Ty. "That all fits. What do we do now?"

"That's where I thought I might be of the most help," said Aloysius. "The spirit has never been captured or destroyed, but there are records of witnesses who saw it leave the mouth of one body and enter through the nostrils of another. The records say that the spirit leaves the old body as a mist or steam trail, which then enters the next body."

"So if we could capture that mist when it's between bodies," said Ty, "we could stop it permanently."

"That was my thought exactly," said Aloysius. "I don't know how you're going to do that, but I did want to give you all the information I found."

"Thank you so much, Aloysius," said Ty. "We'll find a way, I hope."

Aloysius stepped back toward the king and queen as Criseda took off.

As they flew, Ty and Esme talked with Wilhelmina. Wilhelmina said, *Some of the foxes and squirrels who were guarding the road to Dragonwind reported sightings of Esme's father. He's all alone this time, but they said he's talking to himself, and his eyes are very different, totally red. He's lashing out with a long scythe at anything in his path. He keeps yelling about traitors and thieves and incompetent help.*

Ty said, *Queen Elicia said that he started to run amok in the capital and that he'd killed his wife.*

Esme gasped. *That's not good. My mom was the only one who could ever control him. But his eyes are brown, not red. What's going on?*

Ty said, *I'm not sure, but if I had to guess, I'd say that The Wraith is a demon or spirit. As Aloysius just told us, it doesn't have a body of its own. It's now possessing your father.*

That makes sense, said Wilhelmina. *If we kill Stephen, will that kill the demon?*

I don't know, said Ty. *I think if there's another body for the spirit to jump into, it will. We're going to have to be very careful.* He shared everything Aloysius had told him. *So we have to find a way to get the spirit out of Stephen and capture it without letting it enter another body.*

CHAPTER 22

BATTLE

They flew on in silence, each of them trying to figure things out. When they got close to Dragonwind, they could see Stephen hiking along the road. They flew high above him, and he didn't seem to notice them.

Criseda landed on the village green, and Ty quickly jumped down and helped Esme, Rupert, and Samantha to climb off.

Ty called to Martha, Kyle, and Jeb, who were walking toward him. Wilhelmina and Paul approached as well. "Stephen's about twenty minutes away. We don't have a lot of time. We need to have a plan."

The group gathered on the village green so that both Wilhelmina and Criseda could help plan. Martha said, "Wilhelmina told Paul everything you said, and he's told us. As I understand it, we have to get this evil spirit to leave Stephen and then capture it before it can enter another body."

"Right," said Ty. "It sounds easy, but I'm not at all sure how to accomplish it."

"Do we know if the spirit will leave while Stephen is still alive?" asked Martha.

"That's unclear," said Ty, "but based on the number of people The Wraith has been controlling, I'd say that it can move from body to body as it chooses. It has forced four nobles from Estrea, along with four nobles from Mlinred, to work with it. I grant you that they are all greedy, conniving men who probably didn't take a lot of convincing, but still, that's eight men. In addition, he's

157

had at least one henchman, if not more, controlling people like Stephen and Esther, Drake, and Johnston, and who knows how many others."

Jeb said, "Drake and his two friends haven't moved at all."

"Good," said Ty. "Here's what I'm thinking," he began, looking at Esme.

But before he could continue, she said in a soft voice, "He's coming here because he wants to possess me. That way he'd get my gifts as well as a young body."

Martha wrapped her arms around Esme. "We won't let that happen."

Ty looked at Esme. "We will keep you safe, but yes, that's why he's here, or at least that's what I think, and we have to work based on that assumption."

"Should we send Esme to the dragons again?" asked Kyle.

"No," said Esme. "I'm not going to run again."

Ty said, "I reluctantly must agree with Esme. This needs to end here and now. All that Aloysius has learned has me convinced that we need to stand firm, showing neither fear nor anger, no matter what. Are there anymore villagers whom we can trust to do that?"

"My mom is coming," said Paul. "She'll hold firm, I promise that. And I think several of her friends are willing to help as well. They're really tired of what The Wraith has put them through, and they want to help bring him down."

As he spoke, Ty saw a group of four women coming over to join them. They were soon followed by Tim; Wilson and his wife, Selena; and Rob. As Rob arrived he said, "We're here to help. We left Angelica and Ralph with my daughter."

Ty looked at the assembled group and was struck by the fact that most of them were from the former mining towns, but then he thought, *They know what's at stake. They've suffered more and so are less apt to let any petty differences separate them.*

"Good," said Ty. "We can make a united stand here, and I thank each and every one of you for being willing to help."

Naomi held up a ceramic jar with a lid. "Paul mentioned that you were going to have to capture this spirit. I don't have any idea how you're going to do that, but I thought this jar with its lid might help. I make these jars, and they're airtight. I also have a special sealing wax that can be added to ensure that it stays closed."

Ty reached out and took the jar. "Thanks, Naomi. This gives me an idea. Aloysius described the way this spirit moves, saying it leaves one body through the mouth and enters another through the nose. If we can position the jar after the spirit has left Stephen but before it enters its next target, which we all assume will be Esme, we should have it."

Paul said, "What if you can't do that? What if it enters Esme?"

"Then," said Ty, turning to Esme, "you'll have to kill it with kindness, or rather cause it to leave your body, and we'll try again. I'm pretty sure that The Wraith won't be able to abide in your body. It won't be able to stand up against your lack of fear, your love for others, and your innate goodness."

"You're *pretty* sure?" said Paul.

"Granted, we don't know a lot about this creature," admitted Ty, "but everyone it has so far possessed has been decidedly bad in one way or another. It has never, as far as we know or as far as Aloysius's records show, possessed an honestly good person."

"I guess," said Paul.

"What I'd like you all to do is to form a tight semicircle here, two people deep, with Wilhelmina on one end and Criseda on the other. Esme, along with Rupert and Samantha, will be next to me in the center," said Ty.

The villagers moved as Ty indicated, and Ty noticed that Naomi and Paul were next to Esme on her other side.

"Now remember," said Ty, as much to himself as the others, "we need to stay calm. Concentrate on your breathing. Stay centered in yourself. No matter what Stephen says, show no fear or anger."

They all nodded in understanding, just as they heard an angry shout from the far side of the green.

"Get away from my daughter," shouted Stephen. "I'm here to take her home."

As Stephen drew closer, they could all see the angry red eyes. They also were nearly overwhelmed by a black evil that threatened to undo their calm. Both Rupert and Samantha bared their teeth and moved closer to Esme. Wilhelmina and Criseda immediately sent a protective shield over the group.

It didn't entirely block the evil, but it muted it enough so that each of them could recover their calm and their focus.

Ty said, "Who do you think you're fooling? We know you aren't Stephen. You don't belong here. You don't belong in this world."

"I like your world," the ersatz Stephen said. "There's so much anger and hatred, so much greed and petty politics. They feed me and make me stronger."

"You won't find that here," said Ty calmly.

"Then I'll make it. I already have some agents here. It won't be hard to turn more people. Humans are such easy creatures. They're afraid of change or of any differences. You should know that better than anyone, you girl who is playing at being a man."

"Your insults only demonstrate your ignorance," said Ty. "Now it's time for you to leave."

"I'm not leaving without her," said the ersatz Stephen, pointing at Esme.

"You're not leaving *with* her, you mean," said Ty.

Without warning, Stephen lunged for Esme, but the group, in unison, moved a few steps backward out of his reach. Unfortunately, at that same moment, several others began shooting arrows at the group. Martha was struck in her right shoulder. She let out a small cry and fell to the ground. Two of the former miners were also hit, but it was the injury to Martha that caused Ty to lose his concentration.

Criseda said, *Steady, Ty. You have to remain calm. Martha's injury doesn't look that serious, but she wouldn't want you to lose this chance.*

Ty shook himself after taking a quick look at Martha and seeing the small smile she gave him. He turned back to Stephen. That's when Ty realized that while The Wraith was possessing Stephen, he wasn't in full control of him. Stephen was still in his body somewhere, which is why he'd lunged for Esme.

Ty decided his best plan was to taunt Stephen. "You don't deserve her. You abused her. You beat and starved her. You're no father, and you'll never get your hands on her."

As Ty had hoped, Stephen started yelling obscenities and trying to reach Esme. But the group simply shifted directions, always keeping him in the center of the semicircle but not letting him anywhere near Esme. More arrows were fired, and a few more villagers where hit, but Ty was pleased that the villagers kept to the plan. They didn't react, and Ty could only hope that no one was seriously hurt.

Stephen turned red in the face as his anger grew. He wasn't used to getting no reaction. He expected people to show fear or anger, but the villagers didn't do anything, even when the arrows were flying. Stephen shouted more obscenities until, all of a sudden, he seemed to spasm and crumple.

Ty wondered what was happening to him, but Stephen was absolutely still. Suddenly Ty realized that he was dead. Ty quickly brought the jar and lid out from behind his back and waited. Sure enough, almost before he could react, a white mist started pouring out of Stephen's mouth.

Then, before anyone could stop him, Paul stepped in front of Esme, pushing her backward. Ty was horrified, but he focused on the mist that had been set in motion before Paul moved. Ty held the jar in front of Paul's face, the opening of the jar facing the mist. The mist was steaming forward with one purpose in mind, and it apparently couldn't change direction. It flew into the jar, and Ty quickly sealed it with the lid.

He held on to the jar, his hands shaking badly. Kyle reached over and carefully removed the jar from Ty's hands just before the jar would have slipped from his grasp. Ty sank to the ground in relief.

Naomi hugged Paul. "Why did you do that? I could have lost you."

"To protect Esme," said Paul. "I listened to everything that Ty said, and I figured if the spirit got past the jar, and ended up in me, it would be even more unhappy than if it had gone into Esme. I'm younger, more innocent, and I have only a smidgen of telepathic abilities, with none of Esme's power to read minds. If Ty hadn't captured it, well, it wouldn't have stayed with me."

Naomi shook her head, but she also looked very proud of her son.

Paul looked at Ty, who was still sitting on the ground. "But I sure am glad you caught The Wraith. I really didn't want that evil in me, even for a little while."

Ty stood and also hugged Paul. "You are incredibly brave. I know I've said that before, but today you did what probably no one else ever would have had the courage to do. Thank you! You shook me at first. I wasn't sure what you were doing, but then I realized what your plan was, and I was determined to make sure you didn't have to have that evil in you."

Esme said, "Thank you so much, Paul. I can't believe you did that for me."

Ty said, "What we should have realized is that the spirit can't live without a body. I'm not sure what state it was in when it was in the mine, but I suspect it was in some sort of dormancy, and I think that's what it will return to in that jar. I also suspect that when the miners dug down to its level, it awoke and possessed one of them, probably Johnston. We'll never know how many people it possessed along the way. I have no doubt that it could sense people who would be compatible and who could be manipulated. When Johnston met with Lord Upworth, The Wraith switched to a more powerful body. Then it just moved in ways to capture as many people as possible, leaving its taint of evil in each so that it would still control them through fear. When it was moving from body to body, it had to pick its destination and then move in a straight line as quickly as possible to get to that destination. I suspect, based on what we saw today, that once it made its decision, it couldn't shift directions when Paul stepped in front of it, and it couldn't stop when I put the jar in front of it. It had to work quickly because Stephen had dropped dead, probably from a heart attack, and if it got trapped in a dead body, that might have finished it off also."

Martha said, "I'm just glad it's captured. Naomi, can you please seal this jar for all time?"

Naomi said, "With pleasure."

They all watched as Naomi applied a thin layer of wax, which she followed with several more. Then she took some cord, which she said was made from rowan, and bound the jar further.

"That should make this jar safe," she said when she was done. She handed the jar to Ty.

Ty said, "Thanks, Naomi. Criseda, will you please take this to Sapphire? I'm not sure what should happen to it now, but I think having the dragons seal it away for all time sounds like a good plan."

Criseda took the jar gently in her left front paw and then flew off to the dragons' aerie.

Ty then turned to look at the injured villagers. "Let's help our wounded into the village hall and get them bandaged up."

With that, Ty bent over Martha and helped her to stand. "I was so worried when you were shot."

"I know," said Martha, "but you did what you needed to do and I'm very proud of you."

CHAPTER 23

Resolution

The next morning, after checking on all those who'd been shot and finding that none of the wounds were serious, Ty went to see Sapphire and Magnolia. Criseda had let him know that the dragons had questions.

Sapphire started by requesting an update on events since Ty and Esme had left for the palace. Ty explained everything that had happened and also thanked her for accepting the records and treasure from Lord Gofrond.

He also told her about what Aloysius had discovered and how he'd made use of it.

Sapphire said, *You were very clever, and young Paul was extremely brave, if possibly a bit foolish. Nevertheless, I suspect his reasoning was correct. The Wraith would not have stayed in Paul. However, I also suspect that The Wraith would have been very angry, angry enough to kill him. Stephen died when The Wraith left him, possibly because he had a heart attack all on his own, as you surmised. Heaven knows. He was overweight and very angry, and he'd just hiked a long way uphill, and he'd never seemed to be in the best of health. However, I also think that The Wraith thought it could seize the moment because Esme was right in front of him. And I would guess that The Wraith was arrogant enough to think that you'd never figure out how to stop it.*

Ty said, *It makes sense that The Wraith could kill its victims, although it would need to have its next choice readily available. I think one reason I was able to trap it is that The Wraith had to act more quickly than it wanted, but I guess we'll never know. You'll make sure that the jar stays sealed somewhere safe, won't you?*

Yes, said Sapphire. *For the good of the entire planet, we will accept guardianship of the jar containing The Wraith. However, it's time for you and King Bertram to take back the six chests of treasure from the mines as well as the chest and documents from Lord Gofrond.*

I understand, said Ty. *You have provided us with a lot of help through this crisis, but it's over, and we need to respect the boundaries between humans and dragons.*

Sapphire smiled and nodded. *Yes,* said Sapphire. *We'll always be here when the threat is something that could affect the entire planet. The Wraith was perfectly happy to pillage the land for its own power. But if the crisis concerns just humans, then you need to solve it yourselves.*

I think the chests and records should go to the palace, said Ty. *Criseda and I can get them down to Dragonwind, and then I'll arrange for transport to the palace.*

Given all that you've been through, said Sapphire, *I'll have Foster, Oscar, and Criseda transport everything directly to the palace. That will end our involvement in this affair.*

Thank you so much, said Ty.

Ty returned to Dragonwind, where he met with Jeb and Kyle. "We need to decide what happens to Drake and his friends," said Jeb. "I'm sure that Miranda and Mirabella are just as tired of watching him as I am."

"There's no need to watch him anymore. Let's go see Drake and his buddies now."

Ty, Kyle, and Jeb stepped onto the porch of Drake's home and knocked on the door.

"Who's there?" called Drake.

"Hi, Drake," said Ty. "It's Ty, Kyle, and Jeb. We wanted to let you know that The Wraith has been captured, so you're safe now."

"Are you sure?" said Drake, opening his door.

"Yes," said Ty. "I just defeated it."

Drake said, "That explains the lifting of the compulsion that we each felt. All of a sudden, I felt as if I were my own person again, and my friends said the same thing."

"Yes," said Ty, "the evil that has been hanging over all of us is now gone. We wanted to let you know that you and your friends are free to return to your normal lives."

"But what's that now?" asked Drake. "The village has changed, and now there's a skilled carpenter here. You know that we aren't the most industrious and that we've done only occasional odd jobs when we needed funds to stay afloat. Otherwise, we've just hunted and fished and made do. But now I think people are not going to put up with our odd-job status when they can get a real carpenter."

"Maybe it's time for you to decide what you really want to do," suggested Ty. "You're only eighteen. You could decide to move somewhere else, if you wanted. I know that more land will be opening up, as King Bertram has just confiscated four large estates.

"However, I'd like to encourage you to look into options in Dragonwind. Wilson is a very fine carpenter. You're correct about that. But he's also looking for more help, given all the building that's currently underway. If you were willing to work for him, you'd have to be more disciplined. He'd need to know he could count on you. But you'd learn a lot. You could learn true carpenter skills, which then would allow you to set up your own business after a few years, either here or somewhere else."

"I guess," said Drake. "I've kinda gotten used to just working when I have to."

"I understand," said Jeb. "That's a good life, if it works for you. However, finding a job that will pay enough to support you that you also really enjoy is probably a more secure way to go. I manage the forests in and around Dragonwind. I do work for Ty here, but he's a pretty OK boss, and I'm free to work in the forests I love so much."

"Wish I could find something like that," said Drake.

His friend added, "We've never really felt like we fit with most of the folks here. They seem to be all about settling down, and I don't much want to do that."

Kyle said, "You know I've lived as a hermit in the woods for much of my life. You can do that also, if that's what you want. You just need to respect the land and all life. I've made a very good life that way, even though now I'm finding that I like to be around people more. But you can choose. The secret is respect—for yourself, for others, for all of life."

Ty nodded. "The decisions are all yours. There are many options, and maybe doing a bit of exploring around Estrea, working as handy odd-job men as needed, will give you a better idea of what's important to you and where you'd like to settle."

Drake thought for a few minutes. "I've lived my whole life in Dragonwind. Maybe it would be good to see more of our country, even if I end up coming back here."

"You're young and have no dependents," said Ty, "so now's a good time to explore."

Drake said, "Jeb, could you keep an eye on my place while we're gone? I promise I'll let you know if I settle somewhere else, but I'd like to know that this home is mine to come back to if that's what I decide."

"Sure thing," said Jeb.

With that, Jeb, Kyle, and Ty left. As they were walking away, Drake called out to them. "Thanks for coming by and thanks for not thinking I'm a total jerk. I may be unreliable and opinionated, but when that thing was influencing me, I just felt totally unclean. I don't ever want to feel like that again."

"I'm sure it was a life-changing event," said Ty. "If I were you, I'd embrace this new lease on life and take the time to discover what you really want. Meanwhile, try walking through this world a bit more gently."

Drake chuckled. "Somehow I knew you'd say that."

As Jeb, Kyle, and Ty headed back to the village green, Jeb said, "I've got to clean up more brush in the forest. Catch you later."

"And I want to help Wilson," said Kyle.

"Sure thing, and thanks, both of you," said Ty as he walked over to Martha's bakery.

Ty found Esme and Martha working hard as they finished the day's baking. Esme was doing most of the actual work, since Martha's right arm was bandaged and in a sling, but they still made a good team. They had added a line of sandwiches to the bakery's offerings, and they sold the sandwiches to the tea shop next door. Both of them looked up as Ty walked in.

"Hi, Ty," said Esme. "We're making lots of sandwiches."

"Have Rupert and Samantha taken any?" Ty asked, a big smile on his face.

"No," said Esme. "They're both being very good. Besides, they don't like our food much."

Ty rubbed both Rupert and Samantha. "They're smart."

Martha said, "The world sure looks brighter since The Wraith was captured. I hadn't realized how pervasive its evil was. Good to be rid of it."

"For sure," said Ty. "Now we have only ordinary things to worry about. King Bertram's going to want me to sit in on the discussions about the four nobles who were possessed. Tomorrow, Criseda and I have to be at the palace right after breakfast. I'm trying to decide if we should leave this afternoon and spend the night with Bertram and his family or instead get up really early in the morning to arrive right after breakfast."

"There are advantages both ways," said Martha. "Oh, look, here come Naomi, Paul, and Wilhelmina."

Naomi and Paul came into the bakery and, with Martha's permission, left the door open so that Wilhelmina could stick her head in. Naomi said, "Good morning, or is it afternoon? Isn't it a glorious day?"

Ty smiled. "Yes, it is. The darkness has been lifted, and it feels very good."

Naomi turned to Martha. "We're here to pick up the sandwiches for the tea shop."

Martha closed the lid on a box. "I have them all ready for you. Esme and I are enjoying branching out into sandwiches. Maybe we can find other ways to collaborate."

Naomi took the box. "I'm sure we will." She left for the tea shop.

Paul said, "Esme, are you done for the day? Wilhelmina and I want to go exploring, and we thought you might like to join us."

Esme looked over at Martha, who said, "Yes, Esme, you're done for the day. Have fun, you three."

Paul and Esme ran out of the bakery with Wilhelmina, Rupert, and Samantha following them.

Martha held out a plate of sandwiches to Ty. "Why don't you have some lunch while you decide when to fly to the capital?"

"Thanks, Martha," said Ty.

As Ty munched on his lunch, he asked Martha, "Are you up for raising yet another magical kid?"

"You mean Esme?" asked Martha.

"Hmm," said Ty, his mouth full of sandwich.

"Of course," said Martha. "She seems to be fitting in really well. She and Paul are close, probably because of their gifts, even though Paul is half her age. And Rupert and Samantha love it here, living so close to the forest."

"Esme is sure lucky to have you, as I know better than anyone else," said Ty. "I was so fortunate you came for me the night my parents were killed, and you've been the best mother ever, next to my own."

"It's been a privilege to have been a surrogate parent to you," said Martha, "and I think it will be wonderful to have Esme."

"Great," said Ty. "I'll let King Bertram know. I think Criseda and I will fly down to the palace this afternoon. It's always nice to spend time with Bertram's family, and I also want to see how Queen Elicia is handling all those children we rescued."

"I don't envy her job of finding foster homes for all those orphans," said Martha. "We had it relatively easy with the few we received."

"Of course the capital is bigger, so there are more people to choose from," said Ty.

Late that afternoon, Ty and Criseda landed in the palace courtyard. Henry showed Ty into the king's office. Bertram stood from behind his desk and walked to Ty to shake his hand. "You are amazing. Everyone feels so much happier. Your defeat of The Wraith was nothing short of brilliant, and Aloysius says to tell you that you must report to him and let him note all the details down in his history."

Ty laughed. "I'd be happy to do that. Things feel much better in Dragonwind as well. How's Elicia managing with all the orphans?"

"She's another amazing person," said Bertram. "I'm so fortunate. She's made sure that they've all been taken care of. They're clean and have new clothes and lots of food. Those poor children had been nearly starved."

"How's she going to find homes for them all?" asked Ty.

"She's going to keep them here in the palace for a while so that she can get to know each and every one of them. She wants to find out their interests, their talents, and so on, so that she can select suitable foster parents. She doesn't seem at all daunted by the task. She's encouraged the palace staff to help, and our children are making friends among the new arrivals. Well, not Ernest, as he's much too young, and Hazel and Harriet aren't much help either, since these children range in ages from eight to twelve, and the twins are only three. But Lance, Raymond, and Malcolm are helping a lot."

"I think Elicia had a good plan, but it's going to make for a very lively palace until they all find homes," said Ty.

"That's for sure," said Bertram. The king looked thoughtfully at Ty before he said, "I now have four large estates to take apart and apportion equitably. I would really like to have you take over the management of one of them, most notably Lord Gofrond's, since his estate is so close to the border with Mlinred. Would you be willing to do that?"

Ty was silent for several minutes. "I understand that it would be helpful to have me there, and I understand that it would be a great honor to receive the land, but honestly, I don't want it. I am very happy just looking after Dragonwind."

Bertram smiled. "Somehow I thought that would be your answer. I don't know anyone else who would pass up such an opportunity, but I do admire your certainty and your honesty. You may stay where you are, but I do reserve the right to have you serve as my ambassador as needed."

"I understand, Sire, and it is always my honor to so serve," said Ty.

"Let's adjourn to the living room. I have children who won't forgive me if they don't get time to spend with you," said Bertram.

In the morning, King Bertram convened his much smaller council of advisers. Ty was also present. King Bertram began. "I know rumors have been flying around. I'd like to let you know exactly what has been happening and what actions have been taken."

"Where are Lord Upworth and Lord Gofrond?" asked one of the members.

"They, along with two other nobles, were involved in several illegal activities, activities that included murder and a child-trafficking ring. They have lost their estates, their wealth, and their titles."

Murmurs arose around the room. King Bertram continued. "Estrea wasn't the only nation to be targeted by an evil presence, a presence that took advantage of these nobles. I've been in communication with King Joseph of Mlinred, who also had a group of nobles involved, and he has taken the same actions that I have. In addition, King Joseph and I have pledged to maintain a closer alliance in the future.

"The four confiscated estates will be broken down and reapportioned to provide more land, and more farms, for our population. There will be an application process for those interested in obtaining a parcel of land, and we will meet together to process those applications."

"Where are Lord Gofrond and the others?" asked another member.

"They will each be assigned a work detail, and their families will live in small cottages on the palace grounds. They will be watched very carefully to ensure their reform. I think that's it for now, gentlemen. I would like to thank Ty publicly for all his help in catching and stopping the true evil. Without his help, as well as the research done by Aloysius and the assistance of the dragons, we might have found ourselves once again at war."

After the committee members left, Ty and Bertram sat in the king's office. After a few minutes, King Bertram said, "I didn't mention the treasure chests or Lord Gofrond's papers to the advisers. I plan to use the treasure to help those in need, beginning with all the orphans."

"That sounds like an excellent use of the treasure," said Ty.

"I would like you to comb through Lord Gofrond's files. You may take them home with you and go through them at your leisure, but I want to be sure that no one else was involved in all this. Oh, my soldiers searched the estates of the other two nobles, and I've added their files, as well as Lord Upworth's, to those of Lord Gofrond. That way, you'll have all that we know about the child-trafficking operation," said Bertram.

"What about all the blackmailers, like Esme's father?" asked Ty.

"We may never know the full extent of the evil, but we do have a lot, and only Esme's father had access to her, so there shouldn't be much significant blackmail activity, I hope."

"There will be lots of changes in Estrea," said Ty. "I'm eager to see how it all works out."

"Are you sure you don't want a bigger role in those changes?" said the king.

Ty smiled as he stood up to leave. "I'm very sure. I like my life just the way it is."

ABOUT THE AUTHOR

Daphne Ashling Purpus has a great love of fantasy literature, cultivated during her career as a librarian and teacher. She now lives and writes on beautiful Vashon Island in Puget Sound. Purpus works as a tutor at Vashon's alternative high school, Student Link, and devotes time to writing young adult novels and poetry. When not at school or at her computer, Purpus can be found creating intricate lap quilts and spending time with her four cats.

www.ingramcontent.com/pod-product-compliance
Lightning Source LLC
Chambersburg PA
CBHW060155130626
46556CB00006B/2646